Greek Gladiator Sharks

Treasure Rebels Adventure Novella, Volume 5

Gerard Doris

Published by Gerard Doris, 2023.

This is a work of fiction. Similarities to real people, places, or events are entirely coincidental.

GREEK GLADIATOR SHARKS

First edition. September 8, 2023.

Copyright © 2023 Gerard Doris.

ISBN: 979-8223780892

Written by Gerard Doris.

Also by Gerard Doris

Treasure Rebels Adventure Novella
Nile River Scorpion
Congo Spider Fangs
Amazon Swamp Victory
India Yeti Pirates
Greek Gladiator Sharks

Standalone
Wrath of the Renegades

Watch for more at https://gerarddoristhrillers.com.

Table of Contents

PROLOGUE: COPPER SHADES

(Over Five Months Ago – Isolated Greek Islands – Shark Infested Waters)

The green glider slowly circled above the sunlit cliffs before curving out towards the Aegean Sea. Victoria admired the incredible view for a full minute as she steered while sitting comfortably in the harness.

Her watch beeped. It was time to head back and she carefully turned the glider towards the nearest island's secluded sandy beach.

The glider descended right on course until a gust of wind suddenly struck from the left. Before she could react another gust hit from the opposite direction. The glider rocketed from side to side for a second but she expertly regained control. But as the beach drew close she looked down at the passing sea... to see her expensive digital camera hitting the water and sinking from view. It must have broken away as the glider was shaken. She sighed in disgust at herself for not having taken the time to properly and safely secure the camera.

She then quickly remembered the camera was waterproof. Plus the light coloured Aegean waters were still and peaceful giving the impression that diving to recover the expensive camera would be easy.

But she knew better. These waters were shark infested.

She shook her head in defeat and quickly put the thought of the lost camera out of her mind. Within moments her feet touched down and she slowed the glider to a comfortable stop fifty feet from her purple jeep.

Victoria Desmond was a native of Greece and professional wildlife photographer. With her short curly brown hair, sun tanned skin and freckled face, it was clear the twenty-five year old had spent thousands of hours in the sun trying to get that perfect shot.

Her boyfriend was waving to her on the beach. She saw him and jumped three feet into the air and right into his arms. They had only been dating for two months but it had been the happiest two months of each of their lives.

"Something fell from your glider, you should check your gear to make sure it's nothin' important."

"Only my camera Maddox."

"Ain't that one waterproof? You can still fish it out."

"I'll get a new one!"

"But what about the photos for your contest?"

"If there was a memory card in it, they would be older pictures I don't need."

She looked out at the sea and her beautiful smile vanished before she continued, "You know the waters around here are the most dangerous for sharks in Europe. I don't want you scuba diving trying to find that camera just for me."

Maddox Tarver shook his head and smiled, "I won't."

She then pointed to a white yacht with blue trim two hundred yards offshore, the words *Wild Adventure* painted on the hull.

"Or Travis and Amber. They won't either!"

"They won't."

She turned away from the water and pointed at his face, her smile returning.

"One other thing."

"What?"

"You look much more handsome with sunglasses."

He grinned and threw the cheap plastic shades with the dark green rims into the sand, revealing his intense yet cheerful blue eyes. "No way. Already tired of them."

She kissed him then replied, "I don't blame you. When all those reporters take your picture it would be a shame to hide those handsome eyes."

"All they will want to take photos of will be the treasure."

Together they then dismantled the glider and put it into the back of the old jeep. Victoria then jumped into the front seat and looked out again towards the Treasure Rebels' yacht.

"They're picking you up here?"

He pointed to a small dinghy pulled ashore. "I'm to meet them in ten minutes."

She closed the driver's door and asked, "See you Friday at our spot in Crete?"

"Then to the press conference."

"Great! I can't wait to see those Greek statues made of silver!"

She blew him another kiss then spun the jeep away, beeping the horn and waving goodbye through the driver's window. Maddox waved back and watched the off-roader leave the beach.

He walked over to the dingy and pulled it into the clear turquoise water, then grasped the engine cord.

He hesitated.

Maddox knew the "Greek Gladiator Shark" waters were a four mile patch of the Aegean Sea amidst a stretch of small isolated Greek islands. No-one dared to swim or scuba dive in the area due to over thirty shark sightings in the last ten years and multiple stories of sailors being attacked in days long gone by. Maddox knew the actual number of shark attacks in the Mediterranean region was actually small, especially around Greece. He believed only a couple of the "Gladiator Shark" stories were true, and the rest fabrications.

He looked away and pulled the cord. On the second try the engine crackled to life.

But he kept thinking about the camera.

His instincts told him to let it go. He'd buy her an even *better* camera, the best one money could buy, and surprise her with it at the cliffs in Crete in a few days.

But...

He killed the engine, grabbed a snorkel, and jumped into the warm water. He kicked effortlessly and did his best to estimate where he had seen the camera sink. The sandy seafloor was only twenty feet down and he hurriedly searched. After two dives he had found nothing but a corroded pop can and a rusty propeller.

He resurfaced and took a deep breath. One more dive he told himself.

He reached the bottom in two seconds and scanned in every direction. There. Ten feet away he spotted the camera resting in the soft sand inside a twisting maze of four foot tall coral.

He knew the type of coral was not poisonous or sharp, and could see the only way to grasp the camera was to reach down from above. So without bothering to peer inside he swam up and reached down till even his head disappeared from view.

His eyes were focused only on the camera as his hand gripped the black frame, pulling it free from the dark coloured sand.

He never saw the white serrated teeth of the blue shark until the last second.

The shark savagely bit into Maddox's snorkel mask as it cut through the water, the deadly teeth easily puncturing through the plastic and slicing into his face. The ocean predator quickly let go before spinning back and disappearing into the jumble of coral.

All Maddox could see was dark red in the water as he kicked wildly for the surface. He climbed frantically into the dinghy, started the engine and rode as fast as he could for the Rebels' white yacht.

Moments later he grasped the metal stair rungs and hastily climbed up towards the yacht's deck. The moment his face became visible Amber Monette and Travis Jagson rushed forward to help him up.

His face was a mess. Only his intensely angry blue eyes were visible. Everything else was covered in blood.

He crumpled to the deck in despondent exhaustion. He quickly studied the camera for a second then threw it across the deck until it cracked against one of the rails on the far side. No one bothered to pick it up.

Amber immediately began cleaning the blood away while Travis had already disappeared inside the expansive glass cabin to call for medical help.

She kept working and asked, "What happened?"

Maddox painfully grimaced at the brutal pain and replied, "Blue shark. Swam right into the bite."

"How did you get into the water?"

"Trying to save Victoria's photos."

She wiped another blotch of blood away and looked directly into his face, studying his eyes closely.

"Can you still see me?"

"Clearly."

She sighed in relief.

A couple moments passed and then Maddox eyed the mangled remains of the snorkel mask streaked with blood on the deck. He then looked back at her and asked the obvious question.

"How does the face look?"

She pretended not to hear him.

A sad silence set in until a minute later Travis re-emerged from the glass cabin carrying a duffel bag filled with safety gear, maps, and pilot notebooks.

"The nearest island that has a hospital is only a forty-five minute ride by helo from here. They'll be ready to see Maddox when we land." Without another word he ran to the other end of the yacht where their small Robinson R44 helicopter was securely tied down.

Amber helped Maddox to his feet and together they walked towards the chopper where Travis was finishing the pre-flight check. In moments Maddox was seated beside his Hawaiian friend

while Amber stepped back and waved all clear. Travis waved back, the rotor blades began to cut through the air, and the R44 left the deck.

As the four-seater disappeared into the sky, Amber ran back inside the expansive cabin to keep in touch with her friends and pilot the *Wild Adventure* towards Greek land.

Exactly forty minutes later the R44 settled onto a brightly painted helo pad three hundred yards from the hospital's revolving emergency room doors. Travis cut the engine and before Maddox had even opened the bubble shaped passenger door two medics had appeared by the small aircraft.

Travis lifted his headset off and said, "Amber will be pulling into the docks soon. We'll be back in a couple hours to see you."

Maddox opened the door a centimeter then looked back at his friend, a look of intense alarm in his eyes.

"Don't tell Victoria."

"We won't. We'll keep the press in the dark too."

"Thanks man."

Maddox then stepped out and was immediately rushed towards the emergency room entrance. Travis uneasily watched his friend disappear inside, then replacing his headset he began to power up the R44 once again.

Fifteen minutes later the small helicopter softly landed atop the *Wild Adventure's* helo pad, mere minutes after Amber had docked the ninety-foot craft in the island's harbour.

As Travis powered down she locked and secured the yacht's cabin.

They met at the ship's rail where Travis pulled out a handful of Euro bills. "We're lucky. I spotted a bunch of cabs waiting for customers at the front of the harbour when I flew in."

"Good. I'm read-"

She stopped and noticed the damaged camera resting against the rail. Curious she scooped it up.

"He said he was trying to save Victoria's photos."

She then handed it to Travis who examined the expensive camera closely, carefully opening it to check the memory card compartment.

It was empty.

He then spat in disgust and shook his head in seething disappointment.

"No wonder he's angry...he just wrecked his face for nothing."

==

(Two Days Later – Crete Cliffs)

The taxi rolled to a crunching stop atop the pebbled stones of the old cliff-side road. Victoria hurriedly paid the driver then stepped out, rushing up the tree lined path until she was standing atop the cliff itself.

She didn't notice the incredible view of the Aegean Sea stretched out far into the distance, or the burning Greek sunlight which brightly lit up the blue waves and the surrounding island countryside. She only noticed one thing.

Maddox was missing.

Half a mile away Maddox pulled to a stop, his Triumph Street Scrambler motorcycle crackling with noise as he revved the engine. There was no one else on this small dirt road and he paused to think. There were only two ways he could ride. Forward to the press conference miles away in the town of Sitia, or he could turn left...which was the pebbled road which led up to the cliff where Victoria was waiting.

He hesitated then flipped the visor on his helmet up, looking sadly at his reflection in the motorcycle's side mirror. He didn't see himself; all he could see were the bloodied bandages around his eye sockets and the obscured form of the chewed damaged skin beneath them.

He *slammed* the visor closed and drove towards the press conference.

===

Thirty minutes later he pulled to a stop on the edge of Sitia in Crete. The entire town seemed alive with excited anticipation and he could see the stage for the press conference set up on a platform on the docks overlooking the water. Surrounding the platform were thousands of people who were either lining the boardwalks and streets or watching from the balconies of the nearest buildings.

Surrounded by their fans Travis and Amber were signing autographs atop the platform while the tv crews were setting up their gear. Meanwhile other members of the press were taking snapshots of the Greek artefacts the Treasure Rebels had recovered from the Mediterranean. There were fifty items in all beneath the stage, every ancient piece of treasure lit up by the never ending flash of digital cameras. This was the second time the Rebels had discovered a shipwreck in Greek waters, and it felt as if every news agency in Europe was there to interview them.

But Maddox didn't drive towards the stage. Instead he spun the wheel and headed towards the other side of the harbour. He reached the boardwalk and drove right onto it, driving past yacht after yacht until coming to a stop beside the *Wild Adventure*. He jumped off the Scrambler and walked up the gangway onto the quiet deck.

The glass cabin was full of scuba equipment, sonar devices, and a dozen pieces of a strange looking chainsaw on the centre table that hadn't been put together yet. He ignored all of it and instead walked to the far corner where a large wooden crate sat covered in diver wetsuits. He tossed the suits aside and opened the lid, finding what he was looking for stored safely in the bottom corner.

It was a small case made of carved wood, roughly twice the size of a pack of cigarettes.

He opened the strange wooden box then measured the object inside with his hand. Then looking at his reflection in one of the cabin windows, he grabbed a pair of scissors and snipped away at the edges of the bandages which stuck out, leaving only the essential patch around the eye sockets. Satisfied he closed the crate, kept the small wooden case, and ran back outside.

At the other end of the harbour Travis and Amber took their seats. They tried their best to ignore the empty seat beside them, but couldn't. Covering the microphone Travis whispered, "The island's only so big, wherever we say he is it won't take the media long to figure out we're lying."

Before she could answer the roar of a motorcycle could be heard and everyone turned excitedly to see Maddox's Scrambler roll to a stop below the platform. The crowd cheered wildly as Maddox climbed the steps, every person eager to see the world's greatest treasure hunter.

Maddox then began to undo his helmet while Amber and Travis looked at the mass of people in all directions with dread.

How would the world react to seeing Maddox's bandaged face?

The helmet dropped away and Maddox waved at the crowd in appreciation. There was no gasp of astonishment, no frenzied flurry of cameras at an unexpected sight.

Travis and Amber looked at each other in disbelief. Why wasn't anyone in the crowd shocked? Then they looked at Maddox and understood.

The leader of the Treasure Rebels was wearing copper coloured sunglasses which just covered the bandages around his eye sockets. The shades had a unique design which vaguely looked like sunglasses a surfer would wear. The lenses were also heavily tinted and mirrored, so all anyone could see was the rich copper colour and nothing behind the lenses.

The moderator began speaking and addressed the crowd, politely asking Maddox to take his seat. To the moderator's annoyance Maddox instead waited an extra couple seconds to continue thanking and acknowledging his mob of fans.

But had the cameras zoomed in closer the press would have caught that Maddox was now barely smiling. And if anyone had been able to see his eyes, they would have realized he wasn't even looking at a single person in the crowd. Instead from high atop the stage his eyes were now looking towards the cliffs in the far distance which overlooked the Aegean Sea.

And the whole time his eyes reflected the pain he felt. But not the pain from the shark bite.

The pain of regret.

PART I: THE SAFE

(Present Day – Aegean Sea – Isolated Greek Islands)

The brutish howl of a large guard dog echoed across the sapphire blue waters of the Aegean Sea towards a secluded beach. The beach's only occupants were a small herd of wild goats that looked up at the frightening sound. But instead of spotting a fierce dog all they could see was a large super yacht sailing slowly past.

The multi-million dollar yacht *Blue Flower* soon left the island behind and the drooling beast on deck gave one last bark at the goats. The Rottweiler/Boxer cross then effortlessly pulled his paws off the guardrails and began quickly padding across the painted deck. Two men patrolling the yacht stopped to say hello, carefully slinging their uzi machine guns behind their backs as they bent down to pet his head. He barked cheerfully to them then disappeared down the nearest stairwell. He smelled rich food.

He passed a waiter carrying a tray of empty beer bottles and wine glasses, and the Captain's twenty-something daughter Tamla, nervously smoking an e-cigarette and heading to the surface for some fresh sea air. He entered the central cabin filled with food trays, cigar smoke, a large bar, and an even larger poker table set up in the centre. The large dog ignored the bartender and the eight poker players, instead focusing his attention on a silver food tray sitting near the door. Hungrily he began chewing down eight hundred dollars' worth of cooked gourmet fish and vegetables.

Five of the poker players were businessmen in their thirties up to late forties, while another was a member of the kitchen crew on break still wearing his food stained white uniform. But two men stood out from the rest.

The first wore tan cargo pants, a cotton shirt, and a grey vest, while years of working outside digging for artefacts had toughened his skin to an odd brown tint. He looked somewhat like Benjamin Franklin except with dyed black hair and a thin goatee. But while the dye job had concealed Renzo's grey hair, his arthritic hands and jiggling belly revealed his real age to be early sixties. His brown almost black eyes were bloodshot, his speech was slightly slurred, and he had to ask four times what the blind was. The small stack of twenty dollar poker chips by his elbow confirmed he was the weakest player at the table and would likely be the first one to leave.

But the man from Nigeria seated across from the archaeologist was unsure. Sometimes the strongest players in poker feigned weakness for a time. But if that was the case, it didn't explain why Renzo had allowed his chips to run dangerously low. But then again, his speech was awfully garbled for someone who hadn't yet finished his second drink.

A bead of sweat dribbled across the side of the Nigerian man's head and trickled down his face until it clung to his chin. Baris wiped the sweat away then scratched at the mohawk of hair he sported, unaware both shaved sides of his head were also covered in nervous sweat as he continued to watch the archaeologist.

A minute later the river card was shown and the archaeologist hurriedly placed the last of his chips into the pile.

A moment later he watched stunned as the cook placed the best hand on the table. The archaeologist was out.

Drinking the last sip of brandy in shame he slowly handed the glass to the bartender trying to hide his embarrassment. He then snapped his fingers and called the bartender back, "Renzo would like another!"

The current chip leader, a forty year old Asian man from New York named Kozan, hissed in irritation while pointing to the cabin roof, "You lost! Go back upstairs and spend the rest of the day thrilling the other guests with your pathetic stories. We're here to gamble."

Renzo grinned awkwardly and turned to his backpack sitting against a nearby chair. With bravado he lifted out a black folder and dropped it onto the felt covered table.

"I buy back in! Gentlemen, in that folder is...my finest archaeology papers of geologic research here in the Greek islands!"

Kozan pushed the folder back towards the archaeologist, "Then go climb into a lifeboat and row to shore to continue your fine work ...*now*."

Renzo took a quick sip of the newly refilled brandy glass and chuckling he reached inside his coat pocket and laughed, "I want to gamble a little more. Then I will be leaving for Crete. So I will 'sweeten the deal' as they say in the movies to keep playing!"

He pulled out a velvet pouch the kind jewellers use when carrying diamonds.

No-one complained this time. Instead every player watched in quiet expectancy wondering whether it would be jewels, rubies, or even rare coins.

Renzo proudly opened the pouch and dumped the contents onto the felt table in triumph.

Shark teeth.

Larger than the teeth from a Great White, each shark incisor was oddly shaped and wildly curved, the cutting edge heavily serrated. The teeth were dark brown and could be hundreds of years old, but the serrated edge looked as sharp and savage as a modern dagger.

Every player stared at the teeth in angry disappointment. Except Baris. He knew what the odd looking shark teeth were really worth.

Most of the players began yelling at the archaeologist to leave. But the short bartender, knowing Renzo was a friend of the Captain's, swiftly intervened. He quickly scooped up the teeth and black folder and placed a single stack of new chips in front of the archaeologist saying, "Captain Megalos' rules. No more arguing gentlemen."

Carrying the folder and teeth the thin bartender then stepped into a tiny room behind the bar. There was nothing inside except a fire extinguisher fastened to the wall and a small safe. The outside of the safe was lined with titanium and featured a large digital keypad and chrome plated turn handle on the front. Carefully the bartender began punching in the twenty digit code.

Begrudgingly Kozan grabbed the cards and began shuffling. He couldn't wait to take the older man's chips. Everyone else felt the same way, except Baris. He actually wanted the archaeologist to start winning, to stay seated at the table as long as possible.

As the next game began Baris took his cards while looking up towards the bar. He could hear the bartender closing the safe's door and the ominous *click* as the locks returned into place. The shark teeth and folder were now secured inside the safe. He turned back to his cards, a pair of Kings, as the bartender closed the door to the small room and returned to the central cabin.

Baris then anxiously stared at the archaeologist's new stack of chips. He figured he only had a few minutes before the older man lost those as well. And then Renzo would stumble up to the deck and pester the Captain into giving him the teeth and folder back.

Baris made his move.

He folded his "poor" hand and stood, mumbling about a bathroom break. With now six grand already on the table in chips no-one hardly listened. He stepped past the Captain's dog now half asleep by the door and quietly began climbing the steps. Seeing no one above or below him he pulled out his phone and hurriedly texted one word to an unlisted number.

GO!

He then continued up the steps hoping none of the poker players below would ever see him again.

Behind the bartender in the small room, a ventilation hatch opened directly above the titanium covered safe. A man dressed in black silently dropped to the carpeted floor. He opened a backpack, placed the forty pound safe inside and sealed it closed. He then slid the backpack onto his shoulders and quietly climbed onto the now empty table before pulling himself back up into the dark ventilation shaft.

Despite the weight he moved easily through a series of air vents. He knew exactly where he was going and soon he opened another vent and dropped into the yacht's large gym. The bench presses, treadmills, and workout mats were empty. Every yacht guest it seemed was either playing poker below or attending the party on the deck above.

On the other side of the room was seventy-five feet of sliding glass doors, flooding the gym with sunlight. He looked at his smartwatch and hesitated. He was one minute ahead of schedule. He rushed across the open space, slid open one of the glass doors and stepped out onto the narrow walkway. He didn't see anyone and stepped to the rail to look down. Nothing but water. He hurried back inside to wait for the next text message before anyone might spot him.

But one person *had* seen him from the deck above. While the thief was still closing the glass door, Tamla was already running past crowds of people on the main deck above before stepping into the yacht's bridge. She hurried past the two crewmen on duty and frantically pulled a wall phone out of its container, hitting the button to connect to the central cabin below.

After a second the bartender answered the phone and she spat, "Check the safe!"

He rushed to check the small room as the poker players looked up bewildered.

Five seconds later the thief looked up from his hiding spot in the gym as alarms echoed throughout the luxury yacht. Another second and the unmistakeable sound of uzi gunfire could be heard somewhere on the ship.

He didn't wait for the next text message. He knew it had to be now. He ran towards the glass doors and the open water beyond.

He reached the rail and looked down. Still nothing but open water.

Crack!

He was blown off his feet as a series of bullets riddled the backpack and railing. As he sat stunned, one of the yacht guards yelled down at him from the main deck above while two more ran from opposite ends of the walkway, uzis ready.

Then he heard the roar of a propeller cutting through the water. Turning his head he spotted Baris at the wheel of a small speedboat cutting across the bow and racing towards him. The guards ignored him for a second and opened fire. Despite hissing bullets ricocheting off the speedboat's metal hull, Baris spun the small craft with skill so its side was parallel with the yacht. And just ten feet below the thief in black.

The thief jumped to his feet and slipped over the rail in one smooth motion. The guard above unleashed five more rounds shredding the backpack into more pieces.

The thief hit the hard bottom of the speedboat. He was free of any bullet holes but the safe broke three of his ribs as he landed.

Sparks filled his vision but it wasn't from pain, but actual sparks from uzi bullets tearing the speedboat's aluminum siding and seats to pieces.

Baris hit full throttle and hunched down from sight as much as he could, the bullets even ricocheting off the chrome wheel between his fingers. The seconds passed, the guns stopped firing, and the only sound left was that of the powerful speedboat motor.

The thief slowly sat up and ripped the black mask off, spitting a mouthful of blood into the Aegean Sea. A wanted fugitive in Turkey, Talib was in his mid-thirties although years of hard living had aged him dramatically to look ten years older.

The pain he felt was almost unbearable. But he tried to laugh anyway. Baris was also laughing, bullet free as well. While Talib undid the backpack Baris secured the wheel and examined the damaged hull. His smile became even bigger as he realized all the hits were above the water line and the engine tank was unscathed.

Talib dragged the safe out and tossed the shredded backpack aside. Carefully he felt the bullet marks. Not one had pierced through the safe's protective titanium lining.

A quiet stillness set in as the adrenaline rush of surviving wore off. They then looked back at the super yacht in the distance and the now barely visible dots of a few Greek islands beyond it.

"Crete was the plan. We can't hack the keypad without our gear in Crete."

"We didn't plan on stealing the safe in the middle of the day either."

"We had no choice. The old archaeologist was leaving the ship in a matter of hours."

"We have to turn around. We're just heading out towards the Mediterranean."

Baris scratched his skull beside the mohawk, "I agree."

He pulled out a map and studied it intensely. He then spread it out across the safe saying, "Let's head this way."

==

Captain Megalos stared furiously out through the large fiberglass windows of the bridge. He had never been robbed by anyone before and he was struggling to keep his severe temper in check. He had just turned sixty-two, and his protruding chiselled chin, thin grey beard, piercing green eyes, and slightly disfigured nose gave him the unusual appearance of an old boxer instead of a man who had spent more than four decades at sea. He unclenched his fist, ignored eye contact with the twenty passengers who had crammed into the bridge, and turned to the crewman by the wheel.

"Call the Coast Guard."

"Aye sir."

Megalos then turned to his daughter, his anger subsiding a little.

"Don't worry Tamla, those thieves won't escape our fine Coast Guard!"

She smiled in relief and looked up at a large screen. A red dot could be seen slowly moving across the Aegean three miles away. She studied the coordinates and looked back at her father, "Where do you think they're headed?"

He took a long sip of strong Greek coffee and replied, "They're circling far around us probably heading towards Crete. They won't get anywhere close before the police nail them."

She took a long puff from the e-cigarette and giggled, "That's wonderful!"

Just then the room erupted with questions as angry passengers demanded more answers from Megalos. Smoothly Tamla stepped away from the crowd and back out onto the open deck. She walked to the other end of the yacht and stopped at the rail while continuing to smoke, her happy smile long gone. Aware she was now alone she dropped the e-cigarette over the metal rail and pulled out her phone, quickly dialling a number.

Miles away on a small secluded island a bony hand gripped a ringing smartphone and answered her call.

"What is it?"

She looked back at the bridge and replied, "Our worst fears. Someone stole the safe from Renzo."

The man on the other end yelled in anger, "During the day? With four armed men patrolling the stupid boat! How could they escape the yacht?"

"They stole the small speedboat my father had stored to make their getaway."

Tamla then pushed her black hair with the dyed red streaks out of her face and took a quick look back. The deck was still empty.

"It's not all bad. The safe has a tracker. We know exactly where the thieves are."

The man on the island sighed in relief. "Good. I'll track them down overnight."

"No. My father called the Coast Guard. You have to get to the safe before they do."

"Coordinates."

She replied with the exact location of the thieves' speedboat.

The man chuckled as he stood in the shade by a large palm tree, "I'll catch them."

He then stepped out of the shadows onto a small pier in the hot sun, where five men were quietly securing a large .50 caliber machine gun to a metal platform on a sleek speedboat. The boat was custom built, twenty feet in length with a low riding painted black hull, and every inch seemed to have been made out of metal or chrome. After ordering his men where exactly to position the gun, he continued talking to Tamla.

"Does your father know what's in the safe?"

A smug look crossed her face. "He still thinks it's just money from the gamblers on board."

"Good."

The connection went dead and Tamla put the phone away. She scanned the water for any sign of the Coast Guard, then put her "happy daughter" smile back on as she headed back towards the bridge.

==

(Twenty Minutes Later – Thieves' Speedboat)
"Two Coast Guard. Both headed our way."

Baris pulled back on the throttle, panic beginning to set in. "We're almost fifteen miles from the yacht! How'd they track us?"

"You sure the boat ain't tagged?"

"I'm certain."

Baris then paused as he thought over the possibilities.

"Check the bottom of the safe."

His ribs burning Talib lifted the safe for Baris to see.

Sure enough there was a tracker stuck to the bottom, a small red light flashing.

Baris instantly pushed the throttle to the max.

The Coast Guard responded with lights, sirens, and increased speed as well, while Talib ripped the tracker off and tossed it over the side.

The chase lasted for ten minutes until finally it became clear the authorities were closing the gap for good.

Binoculars pressed to his eyes Talib pointed ahead, "Head for that island!" Baris shielded his eyes from the sunlight and in seconds he saw the island as well.

It was only a half mile away and featured a narrow beach, thick vegetation, and a hundred foot rock face that looked as if it had been chewed into by a thousand years of hurricanes and storms.

Baris steered straight for the sand but had to spin away...*another* Coast Guard vessel just rounded the island heading straight for them.

He kept turning the wheel looking for a way back into the open Aegean. But he was trapped between the three Coast Guard vessels, all of whom were calling out for him to stop, their lights still flashing. Now that the three boats were drawing close, Talib and Baris could now see that military grade machine guns were also pointed at them as well.

Baris slowed down within three hundred feet of the beach as the Coast Guard moved in for the arrests cautiously. He could still bolt between the police boats but decided not to. The speedboat had barely survived small uzi fire. The large caliber bullets from the Coast Guard would rip the speedboat into pieces.

The chase was over.

Baris complained bitterly, "I ain't giving them the safe! Ev-!"

He abruptly stopped as he spotted something incredible beneath the boat in the clear water.

"What you looking at?"

"Something I can hide the safe in."

Without explaining further Baris ripped open a small bag lying beneath the driver's seat, grabbing a strange looking digital timer.

"Did you use the explosives on the yacht?"

Talib unzipped a large pocket across his leg and handed the explosive material over. "Didn't need them."

Baris quickly then went to work securing the explosive device to the safe while asking, "Can you hold your breath for one minute?"

Talib scowled, "I can't hold my breath for one second."

With the explosive device secured Baris began working on the timer. But before he could finish programming the exact time he wanted, two members of the Coast Guard leaped into the boat and a wild fight broke out. Talib was quickly knocked down but Baris wildly fought back, finally breaking free and jumping over the side...still carrying the safe.

Holding on to the aluminum edge in frustration one of the officers addressed Talib who was being handcuffed.

"Was that really a bomb attached to the safe?"

Talib just grinned mischievously.

A minute later Baris finally resurfaced his eyes bulging with fear. He was pulled out of the water and steel handcuffs were tightly snapped across his wrists. Talib wondered why his friend looked so fearful...until he noticed three shark fins slowly circling the boat.

Upon hearing of the safe and attached bomb, the blond forty something Officer In Charge, Yiannis, grabbed a snorkel mask and despite the shark fins looked briefly into the water. "Perhaps we can bring it up quickly."

But a moment later his head popped back up in fright. He stammered, "Get me the underwater camera and mark the spot with a buoy. Snap...snap a few photos then we'll take the prisoners back to the yacht...where we'll...we'll speak with the *Blue Flower's* Captain. Secure the prisoners speedboat."

A half mile away the men in the black high performance speedboat quietly watched through binoculars until the Coast Guard had left the area. Angry and impatient the tall leader turned to his men, his arm draped across the giant .50 caliber machine gun.

"We'll go back to get the gear then return and dive." Immediately the man at the wheel nodded his head and spun the watercraft back towards the island with the small wooden pier.

===

(Thirty Minutes Later)

The Coast Guard reached the *Blue Flower* and the thieves along with five officers led by Yiannis stepped into the luxury yacht's bridge.

There were shouts of rage as some of the guests recognized Baris, but no-one knew or had seen Talib before. Kozan threw a glass of wine in Baris' face in indignation and was then held back by the Coast Guard before punches were thrown.

Captain Megalos shook Yiannis' hand and inquired rather bluntly, "Where is my safe?"

There was a long tense pause before Yiannis replied, "One of the thieves jumped into the water before we could arrest him. He had the safe before he entered the water but it was gone when he resurfaced."

The Captain stammered, "He..he...simply dropped it into the sea?"

Tamla stepped forward, "You must have marked the spot with a buoy?"

"Captain Megalos the safe isn't lost. The exact spot where the thieves left it was in somewhat shallow water very near the beach of an isolated island."

The Captain, Tamla, and yacht passengers looked at each other with relief...until Yiannis spoke again.

"But the safe still is...dangerously lost."

The Captain pounded his hand against the dashboard causing every computer screen and dial to shake. "How can it be lost in shallow water? Your men can easily dive and recover it for me. How can *that* little dive be dangerous?"

Yiannis pointed to a large screen which featured a digital map of the Greek Islands and continued, "We chased the thieves into what is known as "Greek Gladiator Shark" waters, an isolated stretch of sea famous for stories of shark attacks. Many think these stories are myths, and few ships ever sail there because the nearby islands are so isolated. It's in these waters where they hid the safe. I had a series of digital snapshots taken of the water below the thieves' boat to give you a better idea."

He motioned to one of his men who quickly plugged a flash drive into one of the bridge USB ports. The largest screen immediately displayed a series of incredible images which revealed a sunken fishing trawler sitting on the Aegean Seafloor covered in seaweed and crumbling from rust.

The room went completely silent for a second as everyone stared at the images in bewilderment.

An older woman wearing a flowery straw hat nervously stepped forward and pointed at the images with her champagne glass.

"Are those...sharks?"

Yiannis shifted his feet uncomfortably and finally answered, "Yes. We count about ten in the pictures. It would seem the stories of sharks have some truth to them."

Another silence followed until Captain Megalos stood tall and addressed the passengers.

"It is alright everyone. The safe will still be recovered. There are numerous experts and underwater professionals I know who will find the safe. It will just take longer than we want."

Yiannis cleared his throat and continued, "The sharks are not the biggest problem Captain."

Megalos looked at the man incredulous. "What could be possibly *worse* than shark infested waters?"

"The thieves attached an explosive device onto the safe. One of my men noticed the timer was already counting down as the thief leaped into the water, he clearly saw the timer read three hours and forty-five minutes till detonation. That was about a half hour ago. I radioed in the situation to our headquarters, but our best scuba teams are already working near Santorini."

"Best case for time?"

"At least ten hours Captain till they get here."

As everyone listened with horror both criminals began to laugh, the laugh of the wicked who were certain they would get away with what they had done. Baris grinned maliciously at the gathered crowd then glared at Megalos.

With mocking defiance he spat, "There isn't a diver in the world who can find it in time!"

Filled with rage Megalos turned away. Out of habit he looked up at all the screens searching desperately for any idea of what he could possibly do. The moments passed, the thieves' laughter grew louder, and the Captain remained speechless. It appeared a certainty the safe would forever be lost.

Then the Captain's eyes reached the last screen where the news was playing, featuring a reporter excitedly standing by the sea with the headline: TREASURE HUNTERS RETURN TO GREECE.

Megalos immediately smiled and turned back, freezing the men who had been taunting him.

"I know three divers who will."

PART II: THE GLADIATOR

(Moments Later – Aegean Sea – Treasure Rebels' Yacht)

Gunnar Monette sat up with interest on the *Wild Adventure* as the last moments of the local news flashed across the 4K tv screen inside the glass cabin. His interest was broken by the sound of splashing water outside. He hurried out onto the deck as two divers climbed the aluminum ladder out of the Aegean Sea.

"Your interview with the reporters was just on the television!"

The two divers heard him but didn't really care. They had spoken to the press over a hundred times in the last couple years.

Dressed in full scuba gear the first diver pulled off her high tech dive helmet. With her turquoise eyes flashing with joy Amber Monette shook her shoulder length red hair away from her eyes and turned to her father.

"Great to be back in the water! It's just beautiful!"

Gunnar laughed at his twenty seven year old daughter's love of the ocean. While she had inherited her father's scientific mind her love for scuba diving was completely foreign to him. He hated the water and hadn't even been in a swimming pool for thirty years.

Amber had quit a lucrative career with NASA to join the Treasure Rebels after Maddox Tarver promised he would find the rare medicine her father needed to stay alive. Maddox had kept his promise, and now the healthy Gunnar was helping the

Rebels find the treasure they had been searching for as a team for over two years.

The other diver walked to the table set up on the deck and lifted the underwater chainsaw out of the sheath from behind his back. He set it down carefully then pulled off his own helmet.

Almost six foot six, Travis Jagson was the largest member of the Treasure Rebels and one of the strongest men on earth. A former pro boxer, he had given up the chance to become the heavyweight champ of the world to instead join the team. The press still couldn't understand why the now thirty year old native Hawaiian had chosen treasure hunting, and they surmised it must have had to do with money. The real reason had nothing to do with Travis' bank account, and everything to do with helping his sister who lay clinging to life in a Honolulu hospital.

Like Amber he was thrilled to be back in the water, but Gunnar noticed his impatient grimace.

"No sign of Wolfgang's treasure?"

Travis shook his head. "Covered a mile but nothing. We really need an extra set of eyes. And we gotta search the shark waters."

He didn't wait for the thin scientist to reply but instead quickly headed below deck.

Still standing near the aluminum rail, Amber pulled her one of a kind tablet off her velcroed dive suit sleeve and turned to her father. "Here's where we've searched so far."

Gunnar carefully took the tablet and sat down at a large computer at the end of the deck table. He connected the tablet to the computer tower and watched the screen display a specialized pattern of the Aegean Seafloor.

He studied the map closely as a search grid of ten miles suddenly shrunk to nine as part of the digital map went red to indicate area searched.

"Unfortunate! My estimates may have been a little misplaced. When will you two dive again?"

She pulled off her scuba tanks and replied, "Later in the afternoon. We thought we needed to surface and rethink our search plan."

Gunnar disconnected the tablet and after handing it back to his daughter walked towards the cabin.

"Let's look at the journal again."

She followed him past the glass doors and stepped inside the luxurious cabin now brightly lit with the midday sunlight. Lining each wall were two smoky white coloured couches with a sixty inch flat screen tv on the left and a long glass table in the centre. At the far end was the command console which included the communications equipment and wheel.

Placed on the white glass table were some of the objects the Rebels had recovered from previous adventures: the gladiator helmet and flag, Wolfgang's journal sitting atop a manila folder, the Congo safe and its contents, and a dozen photographs from the Bounty Hunter's jungle "headquarters." Every item was lit up by the bright sunlight streaming through the four large windows, while the old leather journal rested beneath a bright magnifying light.

Travis reappeared from below onto the deck wearing a t-shirt, shorts, and carrying two large boxing gloves. He stepped past the cabin and instead walked to the opposite end of the deck where a punching bag stand was set up, the one hundred pound bag barely moving in the faint Greek wind. Travis pulled the black gloves on, took a breath, then began punching with savage intensity. The broken bone in his hand from his "special fight" in India was fully healed and he was thrilled he could finally punch again at full power.

Inside the cabin Gunnar took the old journal and sat on one of the couches. Annoyed he made a space for himself by pushing away one of the three strange hoodies the Rebels had been given in India.

"Why would you keep these three old, smelly, and ripped jackets from your last adventure?"

"They're called hoodies these days."

"I don't care what the marketers have decided to call a jacket. What makes them so special?"

She smiled and replied, "Dad, let's just say they're not available in stores."

He gave up and opening the journal said, "I've examined every page using infrared light. There is no invisible ink, and only a handful of letters and words completely faded with time. I carefully redrew them while you three were in India."

He paused and pointed to the gladiator helmet sitting on the table.

"As I explained back in Miami, I also deciphered the strange map and Greek words which were etched into the top of the bronze gladiator helmet. It tells the story of Senator Felix Scaurus setting up his elite training school here in Greece, how the unit was compiled of barbarians and displaced soldiers, and why they were amongst the greatest warriors of that violent era."

Amber lifted the helmet up, letting the sunlight reveal the complicated drawings etched above and around the grilled faceplate. Despite the impressive artwork there were a handful of small chips and scratches marring the bronze which suggested it was no ceremonial piece but had actually seen combat.

"Is it possible Dad we're missing a clue or two?"

"Perhaps. But I hope not." He then turned back to the journal and continued, "As you know the Romans loved watching gladiators fight to the death throughout their empire. With their large arenas filled with cheering people some today see the "Games" as more of a precursor to modern day sports. But in reality the gladiator matches were more of a reflection of Rome's moral decay. There was also plenty of money to be made for those who felt no remorse at betting on life and death combat. Senator Felix was one of those men. Due to the complicated politics of the Senate in those days his political power was limited, so he sought to use his position to instead become even richer through the popular gladiator fights.

He spent a year recruiting the best barbarians and outcast soldiers he could find, while he sent fifty artisans, carpenters, stone masons, and others to Greece to build a training centre for gladiators on an isolated island in the Aegean Sea. During these times Greece was technically under Roman rule. Felix's plan was simple, with a well-trained elite unit of gladiators he would make a fortune when they returned to Rome to fight. All he had to do was keep his training centre a secret from the other Senators, and supply his warriors with food and other items by boat every week for about three months."

Gunnar then pointed to the torn gladiator flag Maddox had found in the Amazon. "But the training centre was discovered by one of Felix's rivals who convinced him his fifty elite warriors should also be used as hired mercenaries in one of Rome's armies. In exchange for continued secrecy from the rest of the Senate, Felix allowed his fifty gladiators to temporarily leave and fight. This flag was drawn up to identify the unit and went into one of the battles. After four months of fighting the surviving thirty men returned to Greece to heal while Felix recruited and trained twenty new warriors to replace the men who had fallen in battle. But then everything started to go wrong, and it had nothing to do with Felix's rivals."

Gunnar paused to take a long drink of bottled water as Amber asked, "Could you read aloud again the written notes from the gladiator you recovered from the museum archives?" Refreshed Gunnar nodded his head yes.

He then returned to the table, put on a pair of white gloves, and opening the manila folder pulled out three pages of handwritten notes that were roughly eighteen hundred years old.

As her father read the words of the gladiator aloud, Amber listened intently hoping she might catch a clue they had missed:

July 5, 204 A.D.

Training has been brutal this past week. Almost lost a finger when Rufus smashed down onto my hand with his shield. Competition is fierce but within reason. Every man wants to live and get paid.

My new helmet is art. The man who built it must be both the finest artisan and blacksmith in Italy. Already it has saved my life twice. Once from a misfired arrow and the other from a spear that would have split my forehead into two pieces. I enjoy looking at the scratches.

The training school is impressive. We have a large courtyard to train in, and the stables are just as good or better than any I have seen in Rome. How the Senator managed to build it all, and under secrecy, is difficult to grasp. But Senator Felix is a politician, and politicians in Rome can do whatever they want it seems.

The Senator arrived earlier today with some sort of explorer from the navy. This "Explorer" named Darius Markos claims he crossed the ocean to a land filled with strange trees and a powerful river far wilder and dangerous than the Tiber.

He drew maps showing us the path of this strange river, and dozens of drawings of animals and large terrifying insects. He brought animals with him too. A box full of strange birds and a cage containing a large black cat the size of a tiger. I am still unconvinced he is just an explorer.

While he was touring the school with the Senator, myself and a few others lifted the tarp off his cart to get a better idea of the man's true identity.

What we found surprised us.

Buried at the bottom of the cart was a large sealed jar with the words written across: <u>Spider Poison</u>. Beside that jar was a smaller one marked <u>Spider Remedy</u>. We remembered the sketches of spiders he had drawn and the laughable claim the spiders could jump high into the air and were purple in colour.

Puzzled and a bit disturbed we have decided to leave the cart alone and look forward to when this man leaves our island.

<u>July 9, 204 A.D.</u>

One of the best warriors was trampled by a horse. He will live, and was given medicine from the "Explorer." My theory he is a doctor is now accepted by most of the men.

Getting supply ships from Rome without detection is difficult. Our food is beginning to diminish. The Senator says he is not worried but we know when a man is lying.

<u>July 19, 204 A.D.</u>

Supply ship spotted. Our hungry bellies will be filled and our training will continue.

<u>July 23, 204 A.D.</u>

Bitter tragedy. The supply ship broke apart a mile from shore. We watched the ship snap into pieces as if cut in two. Shark fins everywhere in the sea. Only three survivors made it to shore, and they all told the same story of a creature cutting the ship in half. Had we not seen the ship torn to pieces before our eyes we would never have believed these sailors.

The next morning we found large fragments of the ship's hull on the beach. The wood was pierced with large strange teeth. No-one has ever seen teeth like them before. My fellow warriors are convinced a sea monster is to blame. I believe different. The teeth must belong to a shark, a very large shark, of some sort.

If the next supply ship cannot make it to our island, we face starvation.

<u>Sept. 3, 204 A.D.</u>

The next supply ship was spotted a month later. We were already starving.

We watched with a mixture of hope and anxiety as the ship drew closer and closer to the beach. Then only a couple hundred yards from the sand it suddenly stopped as if it had struck a series of rocks.

But there are no rocks for a ship to strike.

I could not see clearly what has happening, but I could see the ship beginning to pull apart, the top sail already having fallen into the water.

It was clear that whatever creature had destroyed the previous ship, it had returned and was destroying our last chance at food.

I knew I had to act. I am a soldier and it only took me a moment to plan how I would kill the beast.

I rushed to the "Explorer" and demanded he bring the poison. The man was unhappy I knew about the jar but complied. I drew my sword and dipped the blade inside, coating the steel with the poison. Careful to keep the liquid from getting on my clothes or hands I re-sheathed the blade and rode down to the beach with my two closest friends. Together we rowed out to the ship, ignoring the shark fins which began to follow us.

We could see the sailors were stabbing and swinging at something which was tearing through the centre of the deck. As we drew very close sailors began jumping clear into the water to swim towards our little rowboat hoping to escape. I instead dove into the water and swam towards the large supply ship.

I ducked my head beneath the surface and will never forget what I saw. Below the ship was what appeared to be a large shark...its jaws were shaped unlike anything I had seen before...and it was slicing through the ship's wooden hull.

There were other sharks in the water but I ignored them and swam straight for the creature. I stopped next to the beast and drew the sword and plunged it deeply into one of the eyes. The sword stuck and I couldn't pull it free just as the creature thrashed to the side...the tail missed my head by only a foot. The creature's head was close enough to me I could see the sword still impaled into the eye. I reached for the blade a final time but gave up as the monster's head and strange teeth turned in my direction. A cloud of bubbles appeared before my eyes as the revolving teeth drew close to my face.

I swam for the surface and literally stretched as far as I could, trying to grasp onto the side of the supply ship's hull...but to my horror I dropped back into the water landing directly onto the top of the creature's head! The beast shook violently tossing me ten feet back up into the sky. I dropped into the water and yelling for help my friends in the rowboat paddled alongside and pulled me out of the shark filled sea.

Coughing up water I sat upright and became aware we weren't moving. Panicked I yelled at them to row away! They simply laughed and told me to look.

I slowly stood to see the creature floating upside down in the water, the teeth having stopped moving and the rest of the body now floating with the tide...my sword, the blade green from the poison, still visible.

Senator Felix rewarded me greatly, as I saved his school and all of us from starvation. He freed me from being a gladiator and had my helmet etched with artwork commemorating my killing of the creature. I cannot wear it into battle now, but I will sell it when I return to Rome for a fortune. In Rome I will work for the Senator and also find an honourable woman and start a family.

The Senator also had my sword remade. I reminded him it was really the poison from the spiders that killed the creature not the steel of the blade. He responded by having the design of spiders etched into the steel. I will sell it and give the proceeds to my friends who risked their lives that same day by rowing out to the ship.

Sadly Markos the "Explorer" died a week after the shark attack. He stepped on some sort of fish with poisonous spines near the beach. He has no known relatives in Rome or here in Greece. The Senator doesn't know yet what he will do with the writings, medicines, and animals he left behind.

As for the hideous sea creature it washed ashore for all to see...the men still can't decide if it is a shark or monster.

Finished reading Gunnar put the folder back on the table reflecting, "Sadly ironic that Dr. Markos died from a poisonous sting when he had done so much to cure others during his life."

He sat back down and continued, "I suspect most of the gladiator's story is exaggerated, but nevertheless these pages are the only historical documents I could find that ever refer to the secret gladiator school having existed."

"But we also know the school did exist from Wolfgang's writings too."

He moved back to the journal and began turning the withered yellowed pages until he stopped at the third last page. "Yes! Admittedly much of that part was written in cipher which took me a couple weeks to break. As you know Wolfgang prized the helmet immensely and that he found the school here somewhere in the Greek islands. We also know that he disturbingly raided the school of artefacts then using a bulldozer pushed the buildings which were still standing into the sea. Considering the numerous number of islands here in Greece it could be in hundreds of spots."

"Do you think it's possible he dumped the raided treasures into the sea near the gladiator school island itself?"

"Possibly. But the ten mile area of open sea I mapped out from studying the journal and artefacts you three obtained in the Congo and Amazon makes more sense."

Gunnar then turned to another worn page and continued, "Wolfgang writes bitterly that he didn't find the helmet in the abandoned buildings of the gladiator school, but that the man the Bounty Hunter was searching for found it instead in Italy."

Amber grinned, "The unstoppable Rainforest Rogue!"

"Indeed! I discovered the Rogue was the one who hid it inside the underwater diver's helmet. Wolfgang writes how even he was almost fooled by the deception, but he discovered the helmet at the border. As you know the Rainforest Rogue somehow got the helmet back, only to have the Bounty Hunter steal it from him, which led to their famous and rather quite nasty battle in the Amazon in the 50's. The helmet stayed there in the jungle for decades until Maddox found it."

Gunnar took another sip of water and continued, "I still think it's a miracle you three made it out of the Amazon. That Bragard fellow who nearly killed all of you is a monster."

Amber thought back on the Rebels' adventure in the Amazon and replied, "Thankfully he was so crazy about the helmet we were able to use that against him."

Gunnar tapped a few keys on a silver laptop and a newspaper article from Rio De Janeiro appeared on the screen, with an image of Hector Bragard and the headline: UNDERWORLD CRIMINAL CAUGHT BY POLICE. FAMOUS TREASURE HUNTERS AID IN ARREST.

"I've never seen a more frightening looking person."

Amber leaned over the table and glimpsing the photo said, "He's even freakier looking in real life."

"The kind of people you three cross never stops surprising me."

"I'm still surprised the helmet was just sitting in the jungle all those years before we came along. You'd think the Rainforest Rogue would have returned to the Amazon and retrieve it in the 60's."

"I agree. But there's no evidence right up to his death in Australia that he ever intended to return to the jungle to pick it up."

She answered sombrely, "After all he did during the war it's so sad how he died."

"Actually his death might not have been an accident."

She looked up in shock.

"*What*? We're certain the Rogue died in a plane crash over the Australian mountains."

"Yes but I discovered he wasn't alone on the plane."

"When did you find this out?"

"Just yesterday. Having finished my study of the helmet and journal I decided to re-examine the old flight documents I was given from my friend who works in the military. I had a few follow up questions, and he was able to email me some newly discovered papers from the Australian authorities."

He tapped a few keys on the laptop and a printer below the table came to life, spitting out five pages of records and reports from 1970's Australia.

"See? They found three bodies in the burnt wreckage. DNA tests proved the body in the pilot's seat was the Rainforest Rogue. A private ceremony celebrating his efforts was conducted behind closed doors. A few delegates from

France and Holland attended out of respect for everything he did helping their Resistance efforts during the War."

He turned to the next page. "Here's the flight manifest. See the two names? Tyson and Creggs."

"So they must have been the other two bodies on the plane."

"Most likely."

"But if they died along with the Rogue why would that be murder? I thought the initial reports said one engine failed causing the crash."

Gunnar peered closely at the next page, a police report, "The Rainforest Rogue's body was found with two bullets inside the left shoulder. Another seven bullets were found buried in the rubble of the right engine."

Amber looked at her father uneasily. "So you think they shot the Rogue then shot the engine to pieces? But why would they do that and end up killing themselves?"

"The bullets in the Rogue were different in caliber than the ones in the right engine. The police also found charred parachutes attached to the other two bodies. My guess is there was a gun fight which the Rogue clearly lost, some stray bullets hit the engine, and Creggs and Tyson we're overcome with fumes and collapsed inside the plane before they could jump to safety."

The last two pages were photographs from the late 1930's. "These are the only known pictures of Tyson and Creggs."

The first black and white photo showed Creggs to be a man in his late forties with short blond hair, blue eyes, and a crooked chiselled jawline that gave the man a strange permanent sneer. Tyson was over fifty in the second photo, had long scraggly black hair, a small thin moustache, and the sunken bony face of a man who appeared to have not eaten in weeks.

"No last names?"

Gunnar shook his head. "They are close to ghosts. My friend did everything he could to find out their histories, but all he could find was that both men were connected to organized crime in the seventies and that Tyson had ties to Fascism in Italy during the war."

"So it looks like old enemies from the war finally caught up with the Rainforest Rogue."

She then looked up and through the bridge window at Travis on the deck. "The guys will be surprised at all this."

Gunnar was about to respond but was cut off by the strong sound of helicopter blades cutting through the air.

Outside Travis stopped punching and looked up as a large Coast Guard helicopter swept down from above then hovered over the yacht. Two officers leaped clear of the helo and dropped safely to the painted deck. Travis kept the boxing gloves on and warily approached as Amber and her father hurriedly exited the cabin.

Both forty-something officers quickly showed their badges. The tallest of the two spoke directly and with authority.

"The Coast Guard requests the Treasure Rebels assistance in recovering a stolen item from a luxury yacht known as the *Blue Flower*. Captain Megalos will explain everything to you once aboard."

Before they could say no he continued, "You are under no obligation to partake in a dive to locate the stolen property. But please note that our government would be most appreciative if you would at least visit the luxury yacht and speak with Captain Megalos."

Travis began pulling off the gloves and replied, "We plan to be diving later this afternoon right here."

"The *Blue Flower* is a short helicopter ride from this location."

The officer then paused and pointed towards the glass cabin.

"Is the leader of your team inside? The invitation was for *all* three members of the Treasure Rebels."

Amber involuntarily looked into the far distance and replied, "Maddox Tarver is not here."

The officer looked at the Rebels' small helicopter sitting quietly on the landing pad before turning back to her perplexed.

"Then where is he?"

===

(Crete Cliffs)

Maddox Tarver rested against the side of his metallic orange Triumph Street Scrambler motorcycle and stared out towards the Aegean Sea. The sunlight was piercing but Maddox didn't even flinch, the hot rays completely blocked by his copper coloured sunglasses.

He idly wondered if Victoria still lived in Greece. Had she moved? What had she thought when she had stood right here almost a half year ago...when he never showed up? More importantly, what had been her reaction when he had broken off their relationship with a simple text message, without a stated reason?

At least she had never found out about the shark bite.

He pulled the copper coloured shades off his face and rubbed his eyes. The scar tissue around the eye sockets always seemed to itch when he thought back to that horrible day.

He slid the sunglasses back on and stared out at the turquoise water which stretched for endless miles in every direction. He took a long breath. All his injuries were healed, and he knew they were now closer than ever to finding the "treasure" they had been trying to find for more than two years.

But then he thought of the "Gladiator Shark" waters. He had promised himself he would never swim near or in those waters again. He wasn't afraid of the sharks, but rather of the memories. But diving in those waters was now a necessity.

But he still wasn't ready.

Suddenly his sombre thoughts were broken by the sound of an approaching helicopter. He didn't even have to look to know who it was because of the unique sound.

The Rebels' R44 helicopter landed and Travis hopped out, quickly joining his friend by the Triumph.

"Coast Guard wants our help. Some fancy safe needs rescuing on the bottom of the Aegean."

"Not interested."

"None of us are. But the Coast Guard says the Greek government wants us to visit the yacht where the safe was taken and talk with the captain."

"Can't you and Amber do the talking?"

"They want the famous Maddox to meet him too."

When his friend didn't reply Travis waited before continuing to speak, observing his friend. Since returning to Greece Maddox's usual spiky hair was instead an unkempt mess of blond hair, his usual flashy t shirts had been replaced with a dull blue work shirt, and he hadn't smiled once since leaving Miami.

Travis finally broke the awkward silence.

"You should call Victoria. Clear the air. She'll forgive you."

Maddox snapped his head back and ripped the sunglasses off.

"I can't change this!"

Travis sighed.

"Chicks dig scars."

"I know the saying."

"It happens to be true."

"Not when the scar is half your face."

"It isn't half your face."

"Feels like it."

Travis crossed his arms in annoyed frustration. After months of trying to convince his friend to call Victoria, what more could he say?

Maddox turned away and stared back into the distance. A couple moments passed until he responded.

"Okay. Let's chat with the dude."

==

Thirty minutes later the Rebels' helicopter gently landed atop the *Blue Flower's* helo pad. In moments Maddox, Travis, and Amber were inside the bridge where Captain Megalos, Tamla, the Coast Guard Officers, and a few members of the yacht's crew were waiting for them. Outside on the deck most of the passengers eagerly watched through the glass windows hoping to catch a glimpse of the world's most famous treasure hunters.

After a few handshakes Captain Megalos got down to business, briefly explaining the robbery and where the thieves had been captured. He finished by pointing to the Coast Guard's photos of the sunken trawler now scattered across the bridge's tabletop.

The Rebels examined the photos but when none of them replied Yiannis the Coast Guard Officer spoke up.

"The thief was underwater for just about a minute. Considering he needed time to dive down and back up, we estimate he would have only had about twenty seconds to hide the safe somewhere inside the ship. The safe shouldn't be hard to locate for you three then, even with the sharks."

Without looking up Maddox asked him, "Why do you need us? Greece has dozens of qualified professional divers for this kind of work."

"We do not have time."

Travis replied, "*We* are tight on time. We're on another project so to speak. You said yourself the safe will be easy to locate. You don't need us for easy scuba dives."

Megalos bluntly interjected, "If the safe isn't recovered in about two hours we will lose it forever."

Maddox looked up, the bridge lights reflecting off his sunglasses. "What's the big surprise you're not tellin' us?"

Megalos swallowed fretfully then nodded to Yiannis who spoke again.

"The thieves placed an explosive device on the safe which will detonate in a little over two hours."

"Did you search them for a wireless remote?"

"There's no remote Miss Monette."

A tense few moments passed until Maddox put the photo down and angrily turned for the door.

"Forget it man. We ain't diving."

Surprised at Maddox's cold manner but agreeing with his decision, Travis and Amber also headed for the deck outside.

Desperate to stop them Megalos shrieked, "The safe's contents are worth over a hundred thousand dollars!"

"Still ain't worth it, man."

But once they opened the bridge door Renzo burst in still smelling of brandy.

"Do not give up treasure hunters! Please! You must save my teeth!"

The Rebels backed up in surprise, certain the man a drunk. But Renzo was in fact sober.

"You must rescue my shark teeth! And my geology folder!"

Embarrassed at Renzo's behaviour but relieved his old friend had forced the Rebels to temporarily stay, Megalos introduced the archaeologist and explained that Renzo's property was also in the safe.

Renzo hurriedly shook their hands then pulled out his wallet.

"Teeth! You will appreciate the significance! Dinosaur teeth! The safe mustn't be allowed to be left on the seafloor!"

He pulled another shark tooth out of his wallet and placed it on the table with a frantic flourish.

"Look at this treasure hunters!"

Amber and Travis's eyes widened in shock, while Maddox stepped away from the door and walked over to the table. He slowly picked up the exotic shark tooth and held it up in the bright sunlight.

For the first time since returning to Greece, Maddox's fun crazy smile returned.

"Gnarly."

Thrilled that someone had finally taken his discovery seriously, the archaeologist explained further, "Not only does the safe hold dozens of these teeth, but also my geology folder which contains important archaeological data!"

Maddox looked at Renzo. "All the teeth were found in one spot?"

"Yes! And more detailed information on the teeth is in my geology folder."

Maddox turned to Amber and Travis who both nodded back to him. They all agreed. They would immediately dive for the safe.

They quickly shook hands with the pleased looking Renzo while Megalos handed them a printout of the exact coordinates.

Maddox took the paper and explained, "We'll head back to our yacht to suit up and be searching the trawler in under an hour."

Yiannis responded, "I'll radio headquarters to send out one of our powerboats with a handful of officers to meet you at the dive location. They won't be divers but they will provide you three with any other help you might need. Meanwhile we'll take the two thieves to Crete."

The officers then went below decks to retrieve Talib and Baris while the Treasure Rebels headed back onto the deck, Amber already calling her father to get the scuba gear ready. But as they made their way through the crowd Tamla appeared out of nowhere grabbing onto Travis' arm.

"Treasure Rebels reconsider! It isn't worth losing your lives over a stupid safe full of money!"

Travis looked down at her annoyed, "We know what we're doing."

"It's just money! Being famous don't you already have enough? It will look terrible for my father if anyone gets hurt trying to recover that safe. Please let it go."

Maddox turned his head back, "It's not about money."

Her eyes bulged for a millisecond then she gripped Travis' arm even tighter.

"Some old fossils? More fame? Forget it please."

Travis indignantly looked down at her once again. He had recently become something of an expert when it came to spotting a liar, and his instincts told him that whatever the Captain's daughter cared about, it wasn't the Treasure Rebels safety.

"Thanks for the worry...now let me go."

Tamla's attractive concerned expression turned into an ugly snarl and she stormed away. Relieved Travis jogged the rest of the way to the helicopter. In seconds the Rebels were airborne.

==

(Five Minutes Later – Aegean Sea – Black Speedboat)
The mysterious giant tapped the smartphone screen.
"Where do we stand?"

Tamla's angry voice replied through the speaker, "Bad. The thieves claim they strapped an explosive to the safe before they ditched it. Looks like they hid it in some old sunken fishing trawler."

"I suspect a bluff. We're loading our scuba gear as we speak."

"They aren't bluffing. The Coast Guard were the ones who identified the bomb."

The giant shifted the phone against his head and rubbed his wrist. It had been two weeks but he still felt the pain from the prison handcuffs.

"How much time do I have?"

"None."

"*What!*"

"My father got some celebrities to dive for it. They're headed to the site right now and the Coast Guard are sending one of their boats to rendezvous with them there."

"What celebrities would agree to a dive like that?"

"They're treasure hunters."

The man froze, his thoughts racing. Before he could respond she continued, "They weren't interested in diving at all until they saw one of the shark teeth. Then suddenly they changed their minds and couldn't wait to help out. They couldn't possibly know the secret about the teeth could they?"

The giant didn't answer her question and instead inquired, "Where are they now?"

"Heading back to their yacht. They'll be in the water soon right where the thieves were caught."

"Can you delay the Coast Guard?"

"Yes. What are you going to do?"

The giant smirked and replied chillingly, "Make sure I'm the only one who will open that safe."

PART III: SHARK INFESTED RUINS

(Forty Minutes Later – "Wild Adventure" Yacht)

Gunnar cut the engine power as the *Wild Adventure* slid to a stop a hundred yards from where the thieves had been caught. He then grabbed a paper which had just come through the fax machine and walked out to the deck where Maddox, Travis, and Amber were just about ready to dive.

Each treasure hunter was now wearing their specialty scuba gear which included flashlights strapped to their arms and their sleek silver coloured dive tanks which reflected the early afternoon sun. Each Rebel was also testing their dive helmets which included lenses with informational screens built in, an intercom system, and an emergency air supply of five minutes if the tanks became unusable.

Gunnar studied the paper and lifted it up to show them. "The Coast Guard just sent us a very rough sketch of the thief's timer. I'm certain your tablet should be able to diffuse it." Amber grinned and secured her one-in-a-million waterproof tablet to her velcroed sleeve.

Gunnar handed her the paper then sharply turned towards the table on deck which was now covered in a large blue tarp.

"You three mustn't forget your tools!"

With a sense of pride he grabbed the tarp's edge and flung the plastic covering away...revealing the Treasure Rebels signature red trigger underwater chainsaws and a metal briefcase.

Except now the chainsaws had been redesigned with stronger frames and with each chiselled chain reshaped to have more spiked teeth. Also above the red trigger was a new black switch. Gunnar handed one of the chainsaws to Maddox explaining, "Works the same as before, except when you turn the new switch above the trigger to the ON position, the bits begin to heat up providing more cutting strength. Only use the heat function for a maximum of three minutes or you risk burning out the new engine."

He then opened the metal briefcase. Inside were six small canisters that looked like grenades, except with two switches but no pin.

Gunnar explained, "Shark repellent. You hold the device like this and push the first switch. Out shoots enough repellent underwater to cover a hundred feet before running empty. One time use. The chemical formula of the repellent is environmentally friendly and non-toxic, so it won't pollute the water or hurt any fish. But it is *extremely strong*, so much so that any shark that comes near it should more than leave you alone."

He then pressed the second switch.

Out slid four metal spikes from inside the canister, while a foot long steel rod popped out to serve as a handle. The canister now looked like a medieval mace.

"With the spikes and handle you can secure the canister to a stone or object if you need to keep the sharks away from a specific location. Just make sure to secure the canister before hitting the other switch and releasing the foul repellent."

"How long will it last?"

"Roughly five to ten minutes before it is dissolves away Maddox."

Travis swung the "mace" through the air commenting, "What do you call it?"

"I haven't given it a name."

"Let's call them Treasure Rebel Maces!"

Happily each of the Rebels clipped two of the exotic canisters onto their dive belts and secured the chainsaws into the scabbards behind their backs.

"Thanks Dad." "Thanks Dr. Monette." "Cool."

The phone beside the wheel began ringing sharply and Gunnar ran into the cabin calling back, "That is probably the Coast Guard. Wait till I check with them!"

As they waited patiently on deck Amber broke the news about the Rainforest Rogue while Maddox and Travis made their final equipment checks.

"Guys, my dad found out more about the Rogue. We were right he died in a plane crash in Australia back in the seventies, but my Dad's friend in Washington sent him more info. Turns out the Rogue wasn't the only one on the plane."

Travis was placing the dive helmet on his head but stopped in amazement. Lowering the twenty thousand dollar piece of equipment he looked at her inquiringly. "It wasn't the Bounty Hunter was it?"

"No, Dad and I think they were two goons from the Rogue's past, probably out for revenge. Their past records are almost non-existent."

She looked up to see Maddox studying his own helmet, almost as if he was ignoring her. She looked at him incredulously.

"Maddox aren't you interested?"

He replied blandly, "Sure. Go on."

"Okay. We know little about them, not even their last names. What we do know is that one of them, his name was Tyson, had probably ties with Italian Fascism. Perhaps the Rogue helped the Resistance fight him during the war. The other man's past though seems to be more of a mystery. His name was Cre-"

"Forget the goons. Anything new we should know about the Rainforest Rogue?"

Surprised at Maddox interrupting her she answered after a moment's pause, "We think the Rogue was murdered by gunshot. The two goons were found in the wreckage as well, parachutes strapped to their backs."

Travis looked at her confused, "Parachutes strapped to their backs? Why didn't they jump in time?"

"We don't know. Neither man was shot either, so our best guess is they couldn't jump when the plane began to dive, or they collapsed from breathing in smoke."

Travis stared down at the deck solemnly, "Never thought the Rogue's enemies would catch up with him."

Amber grabbed her own dive helmet and replied, "I know. It's horrible to think he died in such a terrible way."

Maddox finally spoke, "But he died a hero. That's how he should be remembered by the world. Forget the scum who killed him."

Gunnar returned to the deck his face filled with disappointment and uneasiness. "The Coast Guard can't come for another hour. Some sort of unexpected delay, perhaps you three should wait for them?"

Travis lifted his dive watch which was synchronized with the estimated time left on the bomb timer. "We got about seventy minutes. We gotta dive."

Gunnar sighed knowing the adventurer from Hawaii was right, but he still hated the idea of the Treasure Rebels diving without more help. "You three are sure about the archaeologist's tooth?"

"We're sure Dad. It's the exact same tooth as the one Wolfgang drew in his notebook."

Gunnar sighed resignedly again and glanced out at the Aegean. The water looked peaceful but he knew from his research that there was nothing peaceful about the "Greek Gladiator Shark" waters. He also knew his daughter and her two friends were the most qualified divers in the world for a situation this dangerous. But he still looked back anxiously at her.

"Check in every few minutes. Understood?"

"We will Dad." She then re-checked her high-tech tablet before joining Maddox and Travis by the rail. Together they climbed down into the dinghy and powered away from the yacht.

Gunnar waved then stepped back inside the glass cabin to wait impatiently for the Coast Guard. In moments he began studying Wolfgang's journal for the thousandth time.

Outside the Rebels slowed the dinghy to within fifty feet of the buoy, the island with the strange cliff face only hundreds of feet away.

Maddox was the first to completely lock his helmet in place.

"Activate intercoms and oxygen."

Amber and Travis followed his lead and all three stepped to the edge.

"You know, this is the first time all three of us have dived together in half a year!"

"It can't be that long Travis!"

"Yeah the last time was before Egypt."

A moment of quiet followed as they prepared to dive into the most dangerous shark infested stretch of water in the world.

Maddox looked at his friends and broke the silence.

"Thanks for helping me, you know, for getting me to dive here in Greece again."

"No worries buddy."

"Of course Maddox!"

The world's three greatest treasure hunters then jumped into the Aegean together.

Below the surface visibility was perfect and it didn't take long for the first shark to appear. A Great Hammerhead swam within ten feet of the Rebels before spinning away, its jaws visible for only a couple seconds. Three Shortfin Makos appeared to their left swimming at high speed directly into the centre of a mass of brightly coloured fish. The Rebels ignored their underwater company and calmly kept moving forward...focusing instead on the wreckage of the fishing trawler.

It was clear the wreck had been disintegrating for decades, as large holes were visible in the rust filled hull and the deck crane had broken into three large pieces. Maddox involuntarily kicked his fins with fury as he cut through the water towards the rusted boat, his heart racing with expectation at finding the mysterious shark teeth.

But then he paused as what lay beyond the trawler became visible...

"You two won't believe this!"

Amber and Travis caught up with their friend and floated beside him taking in the incredible scene below.

Over a small ridge beyond the trawler rested the visible ancient ruins of five Roman Empire era buildings, slumped over and mostly covered in algae or coral. In the centre of the buildings were hundreds of round stones scattered across the seafloor and the cracked remains of what had been a large water fountain. Over a dozen pillars carved out of plaster, stone and marble could be spotted between and alongside the buildings. Most were severely broken or toppled over, but a few had landed into the silt standing upright and had remained that way throughout the centuries.

The five buildings had somewhat flat roofs and appeared to have been made of fine stone and ancient concrete. One building stood out due to its larger size and featured a second storey, stone steps, and small pillars at the front doorway. But the building was also spilt right in half, the sunlight shining down from the water above illuminating every open room and staircase inside. The other half of the stone building was nowhere to be seen.

The pillars and stone buildings cast shadows across numerous parts of the ancient site, and whatever structures lay at the opposite end were still shrouded in darkness from the Rebels current vantage point.

Amber began taking photos with her tablet saying excitedly, "It must be the gladiator school! No wonder no-one has seen it, it's been lying on the seafloor in the one spot in the Aegean considered too dangerous to dive and search!"

"That means the island above is the one the Senator used for his school almost two thousand years ago."

"Yes, no wonder the buildings are all smashed up...they're the ones Wolfgang bulldozed into the sea decades ago Maddox!"

They studied the incredible ruins in silence until Travis spoke uneasily.

"You both notice what I see?"

"What Travis?"

"All the sharks are avoiding the ruins."

"Sharks must be the apex predators in these waters. There shouldn't be anywhere they are afraid to swim."

Maddox joined in, "Forget the ruins for now. Let's check the trawler first for those dinosaur teeth."

They swam back to the corroded trawler. Amber and Travis shined their dive lights into the four jagged holes in the hull hoping to see the safe. Instead all their lights revealed were a rotting tangled mess of warped steel beams and wood that had almost completely disintegrated. Based on the corrosion it looked as if the trawler had been underwater for over a decade.

Maddox instead swam around the ghostly looking vessel and aimed his light through the empty window frames into the old wheelhouse. Except for a tattered and rotted map of the Mediterranean Sea that had somehow remained pinned to a wall, the spooky wheelhouse was empty.

Amber turned away and looked towards the ancient pillars and buildings. "They must have dumped the safe in the ruins instead guys."

The three treasure hunters swam over the ridge and down the short embankment into the eerie ruins, approaching the cracked fountain bowl and the crumbled remains of the first building thirty feet to their left. As they continued forward two agile Blue Sharks and the same Great Hammerhead unnervingly decided to follow them into the ruins from behind, their short jaws which never seemed to close only forty feet from the black fins on their feet.

But after ten seconds the three sharks gave up following and instead chose to watch the Rebels from a distance, lazily circling the tops of the pillars fifty feet above.

"Okay guys, where would you hide a small safe if you only had a matter of seconds?"

Travis warily looked up at the sharks, "I'd just dump it in one of those rooms and get the heck out of here."

Amber swam over to the small building and shined her dive light through the empty frame where the bronze door had once stood. Nothing was to be seen but two empty rooms and the crumpled pieces of what had been an old stone table. She shook her head, "Too easy. Maybe inside the water fountain?"

But when they looked inside the uneven cracked bowl there was nothing but seaweed and a slow moving Sea Urchin crawling along the tarnished bottom.

Maddox shone his light over the rotted small frame of what had perhaps been the gladiator's barracks, the first building on the right side of the courtyard. Kicking his fins until he was parallel with the crumbled concrete slabs he looked inside.

Nothing. One sweep of the flashlight revealed the rest of the building was an impenetrable mess of mould covered cracked stones, coral, seaweed and brick walls that had crumbled inward.

Suddenly Travis' voice crackled through his helmet's intercom, "Have a look at the armoury."

Maddox looked back to see Travis and Amber waving at him on the other side at the entrance to another Roman building. Travis lifted what appeared to be a strange looking gun and continued, "I didn't realize gladiators used Lugers." Watching the Blue Sharks carefully as they circled above him, Maddox hurriedly swam across to join them.

He took the old handgun from Travis and examined it. There was no bullet clip, the trigger was missing, and the handle was deeply rusted. With no hesitation Maddox tossed the reviled weapon from WW2 away.

Amber shined her light past the open warped door into the armoury's dark interior. Her light revealed a large room filled with mostly empty shelves and one rusty Gladius sword that had broken in half and was missing most of the discoloured handle.

But that was the only weapon from ancient times. Instead scattered across the room were a couple of Nazi infantry steel helmets, a broken wrench from the nineteen-forties, and two black German MP43 machine guns snarled between the corroded bars of an upside down iron rack.

"Forget the weapons."

Amber and Travis turned at Maddox's words as the leader of the Treasure Rebels swam into the room while pointing his light at the wall above one of the shelves. "Check out the gladiator mosaic."

They followed his light to see a brightly coloured mosaic ten feet wide and four feet high made up of thousands of small coloured glass and stone squares secured to the deteriorating wall. Half of the mosaic was missing, having been ripped or chiselled away long ago. What remained depicted unknown soldiers fighting on horseback on a beach.

Amber admired the olden craftsmanship and protested, "Why would Wolfgang push the building into the sea and leave half of such a beautiful mosaic inside?"

Maddox replied simply, "I don't know." He then studied the thousands of small squares closely to see if there was a hidden compartment behind the wall. Amber understood immediately what he was doing and she quickly hovered her tablet across the timeworn work of art. After a second the tablet beeped.

"Sorry Maddox, the wall is solid."

Frustrated he looked at his dive watch. "Sixty-one minutes left to find the safe."

They left the armoury and swam forward until they paused in front of the building that had been torn apart, one half completely missing. They paused to look up. The Blue Sharks appeared to have lost interest and were now swimming closer to the surface, while the Great Hammerhead still circled lazily near the tops of the pillars, its iconic hammer shaped head casting a peculiar shadow on the ancient Roman building before them.

Amber kicked her fins and calmly positioned herself where the roof would have been. With the bright light pouring down there was no need for any dive light as visibility was perfect. Meanwhile Maddox and Travis swam over the steps on the ground level and looked inside.

There was nothing to see but a series of rooms that had no ceiling, and winding staircases that were missing steps or which led to rooms that had drifted away. What appeared to have been a wine cellar could also be seen, complete with broken clay amphorae and glass goblets that had last been used by Roman warriors almost two millennia ago.

But no trace of the titanium safe.

With a clear view there was no need to swim inside to look closer, and with the building in such poor shape it didn't take much to imagine the whole structure collapsing on one of them. Amber tapped a special button on the bottom of her dive helmet which opened the intercom system back to the yacht.

"Dad, I'm checking in. No sign of the safe yet. We've got about an hour left."

"Shark situation?"

She looked up.

"Just a couple Blue Sharks and a Hammerhead who seem rather afraid of us."

As she talked Travis and Maddox studied the entire surroundings from their new vantage point. From here they could finally see the other end of the ruins, where another Roman building rested in the silt hundreds of feet away. They could see it was also two stories in height and had stone steps and pillars at the front, but featured a balcony twenty feet above the front door.

"Think they dumped the safe all the way down there?"

Maddox eyed the last building on their right. "Let's check the stables first."

He then swam across and paused at the entrance to the stables. The insides of the ancient building were covered in shadows due to the tiled roof blocking most of the sunlight.

He then pressed one of the buttons atop the dive goggles in his helmet. Instantly the rims were illuminated with bright light. Cautiously he tested the strength of the old roof with one hand. The structure *seemed* sturdy. Travis swam up beside him eyeing the small boulders and packs of rubble resting atop the roof tiles. "Not exactly up to the safety code." Maddox unsheathed the dive knife strapped to his leg and said, "We don't have time. I'm going in. Let me know if the roof starts moving."

Travis just nodded his head in understanding. Finding the shark teeth would be of critical help in locating the "treasure" they had been searching for two years to find...and if they didn't find the "treasure" soon lives would be lost.

As Maddox disappeared inside his goggle lights lit up the stable's small interior. Most of the stalls had caved in, filled with broken debris and pieces of smashed tile, clay bricks, and broken stones. Tied against the wall were the metal remnants of an ancient horse bridle and an old food trough that had crumbled into a dozen pieces.

Only one horse stall contained anything of interest, a military jeep with a swastika painted on the driver side door. Maddox swam closer to see all the windows were broken or missing and most of the back bumper and wheels were covered in algae. The suspension was also clearly destroyed as the vehicle sat on an angle to the left, while the roof was horribly warped in multiple places.

He swam to the broken front window to look inside but didn't notice the bizarre looking octopus resting on the windshield. The strangely coloured cephalopod leaped off the glass and twisted its bizarrely shaped eight arms in a threatening gesture before springing away from Maddox like a lightning bolt to hide in the darkened corners of the ceiling.

Ignoring the possibility the octopus might strike from above he stayed by the old jeep and looked inside the broken driver's side window. He could see a third of the steering wheel was bent into an odd shape and the gear shift was missing, while the dashboard had become home to dozens of small starfish. But opposite Maddox his dive helmet goggle lights revealed over twenty small holes beneath the passenger window. Curious he kicked his fins and swam over the corroded roof until he was parallel with the side door. Here he could see the entire left side of the jeep had been splattered with at least forty bullet holes.

Carefully he grasped the rusted handle of the passenger side door and slowly pulled it open, making it possible to see underneath the two rotted front seats.

Nothing but more rust.

Outside the stable Amber swam up beside Travis, her call with Gunnar over. "Any sign of the safe?"

Maddox appeared out of the darkness of the spooky stable and joined his two friends in the sunlit water. "Nothing but a jeep from the forties and a weirdo octopus."

Amber looked down at the partially obscured two storey balcony building hundreds of feet away. "Only one building then left for us to check."

They swam forward while the three sharks continued to eerily follow them from above. But once the Rebels had covered only a dozen feet the Hammerhead and Blue Sharks suddenly changed course, snapping their tails in a frenzy and leaving the ruins for good.

"Why would they leave *now*?"

In a second the Rebels saw the reason why appear from behind a series of pillars.

The infamous Greek Gladiator Sharks.

Each shark was fifteen feet or longer, had an unusually powerful and long five foot tail, a strangely pointed but muscled snout, a large mouth filled with frightening serrated teeth that had a strange bluish tint, and a small dorsal fin atop its body which was oddly shaped. Most noticeably were the blue circles and black lines stretched across its body which contrasted with the white underbelly. Even odder, the shark's eye pupils were normal but the whites of the eyes were a dull blue with yellow black veins. But one feature made the sharks stand out more than any other.

Frightening speed.

The two closest sharks shot like rockets down towards the Rebels, striking with a ferocity and quickness they had never seen in any underwater creature.

One of the sharks drove its head deep into Travis chest, pushing the treasure hunter five feet backwards in surprise. Before he could react the beast sharply turned away, its strange tail slapping against his helmet with such force the helmet ripped right off his head. Hurriedly he grabbed the spinning helmet and reattached it, pushing one of the goggle buttons to pump the water out.

The other shark torpedoed towards Amber's face, biting directly into the lenses. The teeth left long scratches but no real damage. Shocked and relieved at the same time, she swam back to the large circular fountain and ducked down under the frame using it as cover.

Two more of the strange fast moving sharks appeared out of the shadows and circled Maddox for a moment...then attacked. He twisted avoiding the first set of teeth which missed his left arm, and the second which missed his head. But the second shark spun back and chomped down onto the chainsaw handle behind Maddox's head. Holding on tight the beast then shook its large head back and forth pulling the chainsaw away! Before he could stop it the shark disappeared behind a pillar still carrying the serrated tool in its chomping jaws. Just as the shark vanished three more of the underwater predators swam into view, causing Maddox to dive to his right beside one of the pillars. In a second Travis joined him.

Fifty feet away Amber slowly raised her head to look over the edge of the fountain.

All she saw was a set of strange shark teeth rushing towards her face.

Frantically she dove back down at the last millisecond, the shark's bottom teeth leaving a long scrape across the top of her helmet. The twenty foot man-eater then spun in a tight half circle before swimming straight towards her throat. She lurched to the side just in time again and the shark's large snout smashed directly into the fountain, the force of the strike so powerful the fountain turned on its side...until an even larger "Greek Gladiator" crashed headfirst into the marble from the opposite direction. The ancient fountain spun and landed completely upright for the first time in over half a century.

Frantically Amber swam forward inches above the old stones and mud until she was under the large protective rim of the fountain once again, one of the Gladiators circling five feet above. She pulled one of the repellent canisters off her dive belt.

"Guys I'm not sure we can make it all the way to the end of the courtyard, even with the shark repellent!"

Maddox looked at Travis.

"Can you flip that fountain onto its side again?"

Travis immediately understood what his friend was thinking.

"Course I can!"

Amber nervously watched as another shark, this one almost twenty-five feet, swim past her left. Its jaws were working feverishly as it gobbled down what remained of a fat jade coloured fish.

"Any ideas guys?"

Maddox unclipped one of his own canisters and pressed a switch. The spikes and steel bar slid out, giving off the same sound underwater a sword does when it is unsheathed.

"I've got a cool idea."

==

Gunnar glanced up from the tattered leather journal as the radar screen began beeping. Something was approaching the Rebels' yacht. Then the radio speaker sizzled to life.

"*Wild Adventure. Wild Adventure.* Please respond."

He stood warily and looked out one of the immense windows expecting to see one of the Coast Guard's brightly painted vessels approaching. It wasn't the Coast Guard.

To Gunnar's surprise it was a sinister looking black speedboat. He grabbed the microphone.

"This is Dr. Gunnar Monette of the *Wild Adventure*."

"Hello Doctor. Can I speak with Maddox Tarver or the other members of his team?"

"They're already in the water."

"Excellent."

A moment passed then the female voice continued, "The Coast Guard are currently delayed."

"I know. I spoke with them about twenty minutes ago."

"Until then we're sending a backup team to provide security to help you. They will be boarding shortly."

"Security for what? Who is this?"

The line went dead just as the black speedboat drew alongside. Gunnar watched with growing alarm as he looked for any flag or identification painted across the hull. There was none, and a tattered tarp had been placed over a large object positioned near the wheel. Gunnar was not a military man, but it sure looked to him like the shape of a big machine gun.

Silently the six men leaped aboard without waiting for Gunnar's permission. Before the Doctor could radio for help the tallest man who also sported a glistening bald head stepped inside the cabin.

He was a towering seven feet tall and a sinister looking handgun, almost as sinister looking as his egotistical smirk, was strapped to his leg.

"Who are you? Get off this boat!"

"It's okay Doctor, I'm a colleague of sorts."

Gunnar fearfully looked past the man at the other five intruders who were now opening lockers and studying his computer out on the deck. Must be thieves.

"I know your daughter and her two treasure hunter friends."

Gunnar looked back at the bald man with surprise.

"Oh, when did you last see them?"

"In the Congo."

Gunnar's blood chilled. He now knew who the man was, and he was far worse than any thief.

Wolfgang "Jr." was one of the Rebels greatest enemies, having kidnapped the three treasure hunters in the Congo some months prior. Grandson of Wolfgang the Nazi, the last time the Rebels had seen him he was in handcuffs and being escorted aboard a police helicopter. They had been promised he would stay in jail for the rest of his life. But now he was aboard their yacht with no police in sight.

The sociopath ordered Gunnar to sit down on one of the couches as he slowly walked around the table studying the treasured items. He paused at the gladiator helmet, examining the artwork closely.

"So Maddox found the helmet. My grandfather was obsessed with it."

He then noticed the printouts of the 1970's police reports and flight manifest. Reading them over slowly he mumbled the names *Tyson*, *Creggs*, and *Rainforest Rogue*. Having read every last word he looked back at the doctor dissatisfied.

"Disappointing! They never mention the other two."

Surprised Gunnar looked up at Wolfgang. "The other two? The flight manifest recorded only three men on board that plane."

Wolfgang smiled and tossed the papers onto the floor. "You will have to ask Maddox to bring you up to speed then."

Wolfgang's strange eyes then widened in glee as he spotted the old journal from his grandfather, grabbing it with a frenzied snap of his wrist. He hurriedly scanned through the pages before looking up quizzically.

"Where did ol' Maddox find it?"

Gunnar simply looked straight back at the emaciated criminal and said nothing.

"Was it the Nile River after all?"

Gunnar remained stoically quiet.

Wolfgang smirked with displeasure and put the journal in his back pocket. He then studied the equipment by the wheel, including a 4K twenty inch screen that displayed the GPS location of each of the scuba diving Rebels below.

"So this is the communications and computer system you use? Fancy, fancy Doctor Monette!"

He then pulled the large Glock handgun out of his leg holster and placed it on the table...pointed directly towards Gunnar.

"When I tell you to Doctor, you will turn the yacht's communication system off."

===

"Here we go!"

Maddox and Travis swam furiously out into the open and joined Amber beneath the chipped fountain.

Travis spun and hammered one of the "Treasure Rebel Maces" into the outer rim of the fountain. The spikes sunk deep into the old marble and held. He then turned and grabbed the sides of the fountain with both hands. "Let's do this!"

Maddox followed and slammed his own "mace" into the side of the fountain while Amber drove hers into the bottom rim. At the same moment they all then flipped the second switch on each canister, and instantaneously bluish-black shark repellent shot out of all three.

Travis then turned the olden Roman fountain onto its side with all his strength. He then pushed the fountain and it began to slowly roll forward atop the stones, leaving a trail of repellent in all directions.

The nearest Gladiator shot down from above but the moment its snout touched the repellent it speedily swam to the side away from the Rebels, shaking its powerful head violently as if to clear the smell away. Five more sharks closed in on the slow moving fountain, but once the ever growing cloud of repellent reached them they bolted away into the shadows.

"It's working guys!"

Travis managed a quick grin behind his helmet as he continued to push the Roman fountain forward towards the end of the courtyard. "Your dad sure knew what he was doing with that stuff!"

The seconds went by until the fountain bumped into the bottom stone steps of the balcony building. As if on cue the canisters finally ran empty. But when the Rebels looked back they could see the cloud of repellent had spread throughout most of the ruins.

Amber looked at her dive watch, "We should have about five more minutes before the repellent clears."

Maddox swam out into the open and drove his second and last canister into one of the two pillars lining the steps. As he was joined by his friends he pushed the second switch and the repellent shot out and began curling around the front of the building, ensuring no shark would follow and attack them from behind.

They swam up the steps, Travis stopping at the large door while Maddox and Amber split up to look inside the windows on either side.

Travis examined the metallic door and lightly tapped what he guessed was bronze plating with his gloved hand. He then examined the stone frame which was streaked with what appeared to be mildew, covering up words in Latin that had been chiselled into the stone above the door. He then grasped what remained of the ancient handle but the rusted metal came off in his hand. As far as Travis could tell the ancient door was now as impossible to move as a steel wall.

Maddox looked inside what remained of the open window to the left. It was nothing but an open space cut out of the wall about one foot wide and two feet high. Carefully he swam close to the edge and slowly, very carefully, looked inside with his goggle dive mask lights.

The LED lights pierced through the murky dark water to reveal a large rectangular room with a stone floor and a large arched fireplace placed prominently in the centre. Any chairs or tables had long ago disintegrated. Beside the fireplace there was nothing to see but crumbled tiles, bricks, and plaster, a mess of rubble. Maddox studied the rubble closely for any doors that led into the back of the building or any stairways that led up to the second storey. If they did exist, they were now concealed behind the decay and debris.

Amber lifted the tablet through the right side window and watched the screen as her computer scanned for any electronic signals present.

"Any sign of the safe guys?"

"None. Picking up any signals over there?"

Amber looked at her tablet.

"Nothing Travis."

They all swam up together until they were eye level with the second floor balcony. The old railing was cracked in dozens of places but somehow most of the stone had held in place over the centuries. Beyond the railing was a single open doorway that led into the second floor.

Amber sighed with frustration and continued, "Guys that thief never would have had time to swim through the ruins like we did and swim back to the surface in time. Besides, the sharks would have chewed him up. We must have missed it."

Maddox was already swimming towards the mysterious second floor room. "Maybe not. The Coast Guard could have left the buoy in the wrong spot. He might have swum down at this end of the ruins instead."

"Possible but-"

She stopped speaking as a red alert signal appeared across the built in screens of her dive helmet.

"Guys our comms with the yacht just went offline!"

Travis replied, "I got the same warning. Maybe an error?"

She tapped the communications button and spoke, "Dad? Do you copy? Dad? Can you hear me?"

Nothing but dull static.

She double checked her dive helmet was working properly then tried again and again.

Still no response from Gunnar.

She gave up and instead began typing a command onto the tablet screen. "I've got to go check on him."

Atop the blue water the dinghy computer beeped twice then started the outboard engine on its own. The dinghy then moved directly across the small waves until it slowed to a perfect stop directly above Amber and her tablet.

"I'll be right back."

Travis looked anxiously up at the dinghy, "You're forgetting the sharks. We'll go with you."

She glanced at her dive watch. "No time for that, less than forty minutes left till the safe explodes. You two keep searching. I've got my second canister if I need it. I should be back in minutes."

Seeing nothing but a slow moving swordfish far in the distance, she kicked for the bright surface.

Her friends watched nervously and kept a lookout for any toothy Gladiators that might appear out of the ruins beneath her. She reached the dinghy without incident and pulled herself out of the light blue water.

Now certain she was safe they instantaneously swam into the eighteen hundred year old balcony room, their dive lights piercing the shadows.

The room had clearly been an office of sorts. In the centre stood an ancient desk but with no chair, while the broken half of a gladiator trident rested against the wall behind it. To their right was a five foot tall stone parchment case that to modern eyes looked something like a bookcase with empty shelves. The room was windowless and an open doorway, the door having been removed ages ago, led into a small back room.

But Maddox and Travis paid attention to the items in the room that weren't almost two thousand years old.

In the middle of the desk was a WW2 U.S. Navy Diver knife embedded deep into the ancient wood of the table, pinning a black and white drawing to the old wood.

And beside the knife sat the titanium covered safe, the red digital numbers eerily counting down in the silence underwater. They had finally found it.

Travis examined the bomb secured to the centre of the safe's door. "Big bomb for a small safe."

Maddox wasn't concerned at all.

"No match for Amber's tablet."

==

Amber took off her helmet and secured it to the chair, then pressed a pair of long range binoculars against her face as she looked towards the *Wild Adventure*. As expected she couldn't see anyone on deck. She turned the binoculars towards the glass windows of the cabin. No-one there either.

Unexpectedly her tablet speakers which were synchronized with the dive helmet intercoms came to life.

"We found the safe!"

"That's wonderful!"

Maddox quickly snapped a picture of the bomb timer with his dive goggle camera, the 4K quality image appearing on her tablet screen a second later.

"My tablet should be able to deactivate that in thirty seconds!"

"How does the yacht look from up there?"

"No sign of my Dad. He must be below decks."

Travis' voice could then be heard clearly through the tablet.

"He wouldn't leave the cabin with us down here."

"I know."

She looked at her watch. Thirty-five minutes till the timer went zero.

"I'll be back in five guys. I've got to head over to look."

"Keep us posted."

"I'll keep the tablet on speaker."

She then turned the engine throttle and the propeller tore into the water. She didn't waste time and was tying the dinghy to their yacht in less than thirty seconds. She called out and climbed the ladder onto the deck.

She then headed directly for the stairs but froze as she glanced towards the glass cabin.

Everything was gone.

The gladiator helmet, the safe from the Congo, every piece of "treasure" the Rebels had acquired during their latest adventures, even the hoodies from India had vanished.

Stunned she ran inside to the command centre at the far end. Every screen had been smashed into pieces, the wheel had been ripped out of its socket, and the CB Radio was broken beyond repair.

She lifted her arm and spoke into the tablet in a panic, "Guys we've been robbed! Everything in the cabin is gone! Everything! They must have taken my Dad too!"

She waited a second for a reply but none came. Puzzled she looked at the tablet. Two words were flashing at the top of the screen.

NO SIGNAL.

Her eyes then caught a reflection off the cabin windows. Looking up she saw the black speedboat a quarter mile away...and slowly approaching.

Frantically she spun and yanked open a small cabinet near the top of the wall. Relieved she found the signal flare gun still there. Hurriedly she pulled it down, loaded a flare, and held it ready for protection. Without waiting another moment she ran back onto the deck and rushed down the stairs into the cabins below to look for her father in case he was still aboard.

But every room, hallway, and bathroom was empty. Just like above, everything of value had been taken, even the last case of Travis' favourite beer.

She glanced at the tablet. Still no signal.

Hurriedly she stepped into the last room. The spacious engine room.

Everything inside looked fine and the only sound echoing off the stainless steel walls were the twin thousand horsepower engines purring away on standby.

She turned to leave but abruptly hesitated. There *was* another sound just discernable beneath the engine hum. Acting on instinct she decided to check the instrument panel...and froze.

Attached to the panel was a large bomb, complete with a screen that displayed an electronic timer.

4:00 till detonation.

She began typing furiously into her tablet then hovered the screen over the explosive device. The tablet beeped as it processed the information. The bomb timer suddenly began to slow down.

She whispered to herself and kept typing, "Okay, now let's shut it down completely."

Suddenly the tablet loudly beeped three times and the signal bar shot to full strength. A moment later Gunnar's voice blasted clearly through the speakers.

"Run Amber! Get off the boat! Warn the others!"

She ran up the stairs onto the deck and froze at the sight.

The strange black speedboat was pulling to a stop above the ruins. She grabbed the binoculars around her neck and scanned the boat. Five men wearing scuba gear were jumping over the side into the water while her father was handcuffed to one of the rails. She then spotted Wolfgang by the machine gun.

Disbelief and white hot anger gripped her. It had been months since she had last seen the giant criminal in the Congo. There was no enemy she disliked more than Wolfgang. She wasn't alone in her view, as his well-known lack of respect for human life had made him a pariah in the treasure hunting world, even in the dark murky world of black market dealers.

He had been chasing the clues his grandfather had left behind for years, yet he often was a step or two behind the Rebels. But his appearance here in the Greek islands suggested that for the first time he may know more than they did. And now the "skinny rat" as Travis called him had her father a prisoner as well.

She frantically went through every option she could think of to free her dad. But she quickly realized the only thing she could do right now was to warn Maddox and Travis of the danger. She lifted the tablet to speak just as she noticed Wolfgang turn and look towards the *Wild Adventure*.

Through the binoculars she could see him waving annoyingly at her with what looked like a tv remote. She knew what it was and ran for the water as fast as she could.

The bomb inside the engine room detonated just as she leaped off the rail into the air.

==

Maddox and Travis looked at each other in alarm.

They had heard Gunnar's voice warn Amber through the intercoms, and the explosion from above that sounded like eerie rolling thunder under water.

With no hesitation they left the darkened office for the surface. But the moment they swam onto the balcony they stopped. High above them five divers could be seen swimming down towards the ruins. They were carrying spear guns, knives, and other weapons. The lead diver pointed at Maddox with his dive knife threateningly, while the others split out to attack from multiple directions.

But the Gladiator Sharks re-emerged from out of the shadows, the repellent having almost completely faded away.

Within seconds the five men were swarmed by a dozen Gladiators and wild frantic fighting ensued.

One large shark curved up and bit savagely into the dive tank of one of Wolfgang's men, the escaping oxygen turning the water into a bubbling mess.

Ten feet away another diver swung his knife at a shark that had just missed biting his left arm. The serrated steel blade snagged a serrated white tooth, and the shark whipped its head away pulling the knife out of the man's hand.

One diver swung his spear gun down onto the head of a passing Gladiator. The stainless steel weapon broke in half, the shark never even feeling the blow. Before the diver could react another Gladiator swam close and bit directly up into his throat.

Maddox and Travis kicked their fins to swim up and away from the growing carnage in the direction of the Rebel's yacht.

They had barely moved before the sharks spotted them...and brutishly attacked.

==

Amber resurfaced with ease a couple hundred feet from the burning wreckage. Her eyes were filled with hot anger as she watched curls of flame consume the cabin and parts of the hull. She then spotted the dinghy floating upside down to her right. She dove back under and pulled her dive helmet free from the chair and resurfaced, snapping it back into place over her head.

==

One Gladiator Shark swam directly into Travis's stomach, head-butting and pushing the treasure hunter down onto the balcony and backwards into the old office. He tumbled into the safe which spun in the water before hitting the wall behind with a dull thud.

Still struggling he pushed the shark's head away but the underwater beast broke through his grip, its upper teeth grazing his right bicep and leaving behind a nasty eight inch slice.

Travis grunted in savage pain and pulled the chainsaw out of the scabbard behind his back and pulled the red trigger in one motion. Immediately the chiselled chain began spinning in the water and the dull whine from the specialized engine began echoing off the walls. The shark spun away because of the unusual sound, and spotting one of Wolfgang's men outside with its strangely coloured eyes, it shot out through the door eager to leave the treasure hunter and the chainsaw behind.

A second later Maddox grasped the upper frame of the door and pulled himself into the room beside Travis just before two more sharks swam past the open doorway, both of their jaws and snouts stained dark red.

He barely looked at Travis and instead swam like a rocket towards the safe. Apprehensively he looked down and examined it. The digital timer along with the front of the safe was now covered in dirt. Hesitantly Maddox reached down and began to wipe the grime away while Travis released the chainsaw trigger and asked the obvious question.

"Is it gonna explode?"

Maddox looked back and instead yelled, "Seal the door!"

Travis rushed to the old parchment case and pushed it across the open doorway, holding it in place. Immediately two shark snouts could be seen aggressively striking the case from the other side, but neither predator could make its way inside the room.

Amber's voice suddenly crackled to life in their helmets.

"Guys Wolfgang is back! He's-"

"The rat's in jail! He can't be back!"

"He's right above you guys, he's got my dad in handcuffs! Some of his men headed down your way a few minutes ago. Are you okay?"

Maddox was barely listening, instead focused on the front of the safe. He could see the faint image of the digital numbers begin to appear. Slowly he kept wiping the dirt away...pulling back in surprise as the red timer finally became visible.

Anxiously he looked at Travis then up at the stone ceiling before replying to Amber.

"We're trapped in the balcony room...Travis got bitten in the arm and the safe got pushed off the table."

"WHAT! How bad is-"

"He's okay. We've got the doorway blocked."

"Okay. Good. Let's regroup and-"

"It gets worse."

"What! How?"

"The timer got scrambled."

Maddox then looked back at the safe, the digital numbers reflecting off his dive mask.

"There's only fifteen seconds left."

PART IV: CARD SHARKS

"How we gonna do this? There's four sharks tryin' to break in now!"

Maddox didn't reply but moved with laser speed. In one motion he swam behind Travis, grabbed his friend's chainsaw then kicked back to the safe. He turned the heat switch to ON, pressed the red trigger button and sliced downward. The heated chain and serrated bits cut right through the titanium with ease, chopping off the last two inches of the back of the safe like a slice of bread.

Maddox looked at the timer.

Twelve seconds...

He reached into the small safe and pulled out everything he could, littering the cracked marble floor with cell phones, diamonds, cash...and Renzo's shark tooth pouch and black folder. He slid the folder into a waterproof pocket of his dive suit then grabbed the broken war trident.

Eight seconds...

He drove the trident downward through the cut opening until the barbed prongs embedded deeply and securely into the bottom of the safe.

"Open the door!"

Six seconds...

Travis pulled the case away as Maddox lifted the trident with the safe attached, "throwing" it forward like a javelin through the open doorway and out into the ruins.

Two seconds...

All four sharks spun and chased after the slowly spinning safe unaware of the danger, closing in as the red timer finally hit zero.

BOOM!!

The safe detonated powerfully, killing three of the sharks instantly while the fourth had part of its lower jaw blown off by the sizzling explosives. Deeply hurt the wounded shark frantically swam away, its strange tail driving the predator through the water until it disappeared around a pillar into the depths of the Aegean.

The force of the blast reverberated throughout the ancient ruins causing the balcony to shake violently and the walls inside the office to shudder as if an earthquake had hit. But in a moment everything calmed down and Travis pushed the parchment case back while Maddox hurriedly began scooping up the rest of the safe's contents and putting them into waterproof pockets.

Amber's voice crackled in their helmets.

"Guys! Was that an explosion? Please tell me you both made it out!"

Travis picked up and re-sheathed the chainsaw replying, "We're good. Four Gladiators down. What's the status up there?"

A moment passed before she replied.

"Three of Wolfgang's men just resurfaced and are swimming back to his boat. Wolfgang is talking on a cell to someone. I'll let you know when the other divers resurface."

Travis opened one of the pockets beneath his kneecap and pulled out a large stretch of unusual looking gauze like tape and began wrapping it tightly around his bleeding arm.

"They ain't gonna resurface. Gladiator lunch."

Maddox looked up from the small pile of valuables and smartphones and asked Amber, "Coast Guard coming?"

"Can't call anyone. I think Wolfgang is somehow jamming the tablet's signal. It only reactivated on the yacht for a couple seconds. That was Dad for sure. All that work's right now is our helmet intercoms and that's because they function on their own independent system."

She then went to continue speaking but faltered as she sadly watched the yacht sink another foot into the Aegean.

"Our beautiful yacht! It's slowly disappearing before my eyes!"

Travis finished tying the bandage with a snap as he replied, "Don't worry...we're gonna make sure the rat buys us a new one!"

When she didn't reply Travis continued, "Forget the yacht for now. You still okay up there?"

"I'll be fine Travis. I'm treading water behind the wreckage out of Wolfgang's line of sight."

She then paused as she spotted their R44 helicopter still secured to the *Wild Adventure's* deck above the water.

"We can still use the helicopter guys! Just resurface by me and we can try to fly."

Maddox disagreed, "No, I think we should head for the beach. Wolfgang could have disabled the helo. We'll draw Wolfgang's little crew away from you. If the R44 works meet us on the island, if it doesn't we'll signal the Coast Guard when we see 'em. Either way we all beat Wolfgang."

She peered around a piece of scorched floating debris to look back at Gunnar handcuffed.

"Except my father."

Maddox replied his voice full of assurance.

"He won't hurt the Doctor as long as we're still free to stop him."

Amber continued to tread water as her thoughts drifted back to the Congo, remembering Wolfgang's lack of confidence and insecure behaviour at times. She smiled. "You're right. Wolfgang is afraid of us...and he knows he should be!"

Maddox continued stowing the safe's contents in secure waterproof pockets while Travis righted the wobbly desk. Even after being toppled the diver knife was still stuck to the wood, pinning the special heavy laminated drawing to the desk. Travis looked closer and could see that Baris had likely tried to pry the knife free after leaving the safe but had lacked the strength to succeed. Travis pulled the old WW2 blade out of the wood with ease while Maddox quickly put the old laminated drawing of what appeared to be a castle inside his dive suit. "I'll check this later man."

Travis held up the timeworn weapon, "Old knife. Think the Rainforest Rogue left it years ago?"

"Maybe."

Maddox then scooped the shark teeth carefully off the floor and placed them onto the desk as Travis asked, "You really think Wolfgang carved the location on the teeth?"

Without replying Maddox lifted one of the teeth five inches from his eyes in the goggle dive light and pushed one of the buttons on his dive helmet. Instantly the lenses were magnified and the finest details of the tooth became visible.

"Nothin' man."

Travis handed him another tooth while watching the doorway closely for any movement in the ruins beyond.

"How about that one?"

Maddox laughed, "Two numbers! A three and four!"

Travis continued handing over the teeth for his friend to study, and in less than a minute Maddox had discovered that twenty teeth out of thirty had numbers scratched into them.

Travis spoke into his intercom, "You hearing this Amber? The notebook was right! We got a bunch of numbers on twenty teeth!"

"Tell me every number guys and the tablet will have a longitude and latitude targeted in seconds."

Moments later she continued, "Got the GPS location guys! Put the numbers together and my digital map points to a spot in the Aegean about twenty miles away."

"We're heading for the beach now. Hopin' the Coast Guard are approaching when we step onto the sand."

"Copy that Maddox. I'm heading for the helicopter."

Travis then pushed the ancient parchment case aside for the last time. Together they swam back out into the ruins ready to face the remaining horde of sharks, Maddox holding his dive knife while Travis held the underwater chainsaw in one hand and his last canister of shark repellent in the other. But for the first time there were no sharks, or any fish, to be seen in all directions thanks to the loud explosion having caused all marine life to temporarily retreat from the ruins.

Guardedly they slowly swam upwards leaving the ruins below and behind for good. Maddox took the lead and had already focused his attention on reaching the island ahead. But Travis gave one last look behind.

Then he saw it.

Far away near the other end of the ruins he spotted a giant black tail fin slowly curving around the corner of what remained of the armoury.

He blinked trying to be certain of what he was seeing. It slowly disappeared from sight and from this distance it was hard for him to estimate the size. Eight feet? Ten feet? Bigger? He had never seen the tail of any fish that large before in his life. He simply couldn't decipher the species of fish or estimate its full size.

But he was certain of one thing.

It looked like a shark tail.

He turned away from the ruins and kicking hard he quickly caught up with Maddox.

"Let's get to the beach as fast as we can."

===

(Moments Later – Blue Flower Yacht)
Kozan nearly fell over in shock.

The poker player had been walking along the yacht's rail to clear his head when he heard Tamla's voice coming from the open window of one of the suites above. He still couldn't believe the words he had heard:

"You don't have to worry about the Coast Guard yet. I've succeeded in stalling them longer...you have one more hour."

He pressed his back against the wall out of sight below the window and continued listening. After a dozen seconds he could hear a series of more comments by Tamla:

"The bomb went off?"

"How many sharks?"

"Who has the teeth now?"

"I'm going to check on my father in the bridge then I'll call you in ten minutes when I get back to my room. Let's hope you've caught them and have Renzo's teeth."

She spoke no more and the distant sound of a door slamming could be heard. She had left the suite.

Kozan's mind raced over the obvious questions.

Who was Tamla talking to? Was Megalos involved, or was his own daughter lying to him as well? And how could she trick the Coast Guard into staying away?

He took a long breath and irately threw his cigarette over the rail as he continued thinking.

What about those treasure hunters? Whose side were they on?

He then remembered seeing how desperate Tamla had been earlier when she had tried to convince the Rebels to give up the search.

No, those celebrities aren't working with her. If anything, they're ruining her plans.

That means I can still get my money and phone back from the safe, but only if I help those treasure hunters in time.

He took a few long breaths as his sharp mind raced to figure out a way to contact the Coast Guard. He had no phone and he didn't dare try to use the one in the bridge until he knew whether he could trust Megalos. That meant there was only one way to get the Coast Guard to come to him.

He stepped towards the nearest safety alarm ready to pull the switch.

"There is no need for that Mr. Kozan!"

He froze at the sound of the voice behind him and gradually, uneasily turned.

There stood Renzo holding a cell phone and staring at him intently.

Kozan was a professional poker player, which really meant he was an expert in reading people. And he could see that Renzo was different. The archaeologists' naïve friendly smile and drunken body language were gone. There was also now a bit of angry coldness to the man's voice instead of the happy-go-lucky tone from the poker game.

Renzo continued, "I insist that I call my brother first!"

"Why? The sooner the Coast Guard arrive the be-!"

Renzo waved the thin phone snootily in Kozan's face. "Waste of time! A waste! You heard the captain's daughter. They are only delayed from reaching the dive site. If they think there's an emergency here they will come to the yacht first and waste even more time."

Kozan hesitated then responded, "Okay, you call them to explain *now*."

"Not yet! I will call my brother first. If those thieves steal my property from the safe it will put him in grave danger! He is heading towards these islands as we speak, and he can tell us if he sees the Coast Guard coming."

Renzo looked up at the open window above them and continued, "Let's wait to hear if her friend on the phone has found my teeth first."

PART V: THE BLACK FOLDER

Amber swam towards the half submerged yacht keeping a careful eye on the dark coloured speedboat. Swimming anywhere close to a sinking ship, large or small, was extremely dangerous as the person could be sucked under as the ship sank. But her only other option was to surrender to Wolfgang who might just shoot her.

She reached the yacht which was now tilted on a twenty-five degree angle and grasped the edge with both hands. She pulled herself out of the water and carefully approached the helicopter which was still securely tied down. The glass canopy was cracked in ten places but the rest of the R44 didn't have a scratch. She opened the pilot's door and stepped inside, sitting in the reinforced chair and hurriedly checking the dials and radio for signs of life.

Nothing. Every screen remained black and only static filled the air. Whether caused by Wolfgang or the explosion, the helicopter's electrical system was completely unresponsive. She sighed in discouragement and spoke into her dive helmet.

"The helicopter's dead guys. How close are you to the beach?"

"A hundred feet."

She looked through the cracked glass at Wolfgang in the distance.

"He still hasn't moved. I don't see any of his men either, they must all be in the water searching the ruins for you."

"Copy that."

She dropped her helmet onto the co-pilot's chair and began examining the dashboard to try and fix what might be wrong. She knew how to fix and pull apart the intricate and complex wiring of a modern spaceship, so if there was any way to bring the helo or radio to life she would easily find it.

But she froze as she saw through the cockpit glass the form of a scuba diver's head, then his shoulders slowly and menacingly come out of the water directly in front of the slowly sinking yacht. The man then pointed a strange looking gun at her while two more divers appeared out of the Aegean. She slowly lifted her hands in surrender.

===

(Three Minutes Later)

Maddox and Travis left their fins in the beach mud and began pulling off their helmets. Facing them was the hundred foot cliff face. It only took them a couple seconds to spot the foot pathway which had been chiselled out of the stone almost two millennia ago by Senator Felix's men.

As they walked across the soft sand they heard the far off engine growl of a powerful outboard motor. Fearing what they'd see they looked back. In the distance Wolfgang's boat could be seen slowly picking up speed...and heading towards them!

Immediately they dropped their helmets and tanks onto the beach and ran as fast as possible onto the stone pathway and up the winding steps, thankful for the odd rare shadow and tree that hid them temporarily. In moments they were fifty feet above the beach.

Below Wolfgang's black speedboat pulled right up to the surf's edge. Neither Treasure Rebel heard the enormous machine gun being readied.

But they did hear Amber's warning scream, and as they spun to look down all they could see was red white flame spewing out of the gun's long barrel. They dove behind the nearest boulder as a streak of hot bullets began slicing into the cliff face where they had been standing a second before. Pieces of stone flew in every direction as each bullet took a small chunk out of the cliff. After half a dozen seconds the gunner then shifted the barrel downwards towards the large boulder protecting them.

Maddox and Travis could actually *feel* the bullets chewing away at the other side of the immense rock.

"That's a sick weapon!"

Maddox just nodded his head in agreement as he desperately looked for a way out. He couldn't see any.

The gunner finally released the black trigger and an odd silence fell across the beach...until Wolfgang's strange and menacing voice cut through the air by way of a megaphone he held.

"Maddox! Walk down to the beach and board my boat. I already have Amber and her father."

The two trapped Treasure Rebels slowly looked over the boulder.

Two of Wolfgang's men were already on the beach, both armed and moving quickly towards the stone steps. Amber and Gunnar could be seen sitting side by side handcuffed to the ship's steel railing.

The third member of Wolfgang's crew could be spotted waiting by the machine gun eerily watching the cliff through the gun sights. Even from this distance Travis was convinced he could see a malicious smile on the man's face.

Pinned down by the gunner there was nothing they could do. Cautiously they lifted their arms and began the slow walk back down onto the beach at gunpoint.

Every step they looked for any means of escape, but there were none.

Yet.

As they traveled across the hot sand they were ordered to pick up their gear then hand it all over to the gunner waiting in the speedboat.

Wolfgang watched from the gun platform above, his weird goatee blowing in the wind while standing with one foot atop the rail like a victorious pirate studying prisoners he had just captured.

As Maddox and Travis warily climbed up the short steel ladder Gunnar and Amber stood to greet them, both smiling with relief they were okay.

Gunnar then nodded with his head towards the front of the boat where four large plastic tubs were stacked together under the wheel and gun platform. "Everything these monsters took from our yacht is stored in those containers."

Amber then lifted her free arm to show the tablet sleeve was empty. She then nodded dejectedly towards the plastic containers as well. "Wolfgang threw my tablet in with everything else."

Maddox and Travis were then ordered to hand over any remaining scuba gear and empty their dive suit pockets. Soon all of the safe's contents, Renzo's black folder, the shark teeth, Travis' underwater chainsaw, the WW2 knife, and all of their remaining gear and tools were dropped onto the deck at their feet.

But the strange laminated castle drawing Maddox kept hidden inside his suit.

Now only wearing their black dive suits, Maddox and Travis tensely watched as Wolfgang opened the velvet pouch and poured the shark teeth carefully onto a plastic tray.

Using a jewelers loupe it only took the escaped convict two seconds to notice the numbers etched into the teeth.

Wolfgang quickly lined up the teeth then barked at one of his men. "Put these numbers into the computer until a location comes up."

The gunner quickly began typing the numbers into a large steel laptop. In less than twenty seconds the laptop had sorted out all of the possible combinations and found a match.

The man spun the computer to face Wolfgang. The same longitude and latitude Amber had reported minutes earlier was displayed on the bright screen.

"About twenty miles from here! Really remote. Right at the base of a small island. Don't think anyone lives there."

Wolfgang tugged at his goatee and looked in the distance, his eyes unblinking as he thought out a plan. His thoughts were broken by his smartphone ringing. A second later Tamla's impatient angry voice came through the speakers.

"Have the safe?"

"Better. I have the safe's contents, the location of my grandfather's treasure hoard...and I have the Treasure Rebels all under guard."

He quickly signalled one of his men to handcuff Maddox and Travis to the rail then pointed at the gunner to pull the speedboat away from the beach and back out into the open Aegean. He then continued speaking to Tamla.

"The treasure is only twenty miles away. We'll be there in under half an hour, then I'll use the Rebels to dive. Here's the longitude and latitude."

After listening to Wolfgang she repeated the coordinates out loud and typed them into her phone, unaware Renzo and Kozan were listening to every word beneath the window.

Certain she now had the location locked in, she asked Wolfgang directly, "Why trust the Treasure Rebels to do the dive? Why not use your own men?"

Wolfgang's foul smirk grew uglier as he looked at his prisoners all handcuffed to the steel rail, then at the immense machine gun.

"The Rebels can't get away this time."

He ended the call just as the gunner spun the wheel towards open water.

Everyone remained silent as the minutes went by and Wolfgang's speedboat drew closer to the secluded island. They passed no other ships or smaller boats, except for the sad sight of the *Wild Adventure* now almost completely submerged and covered in orange flames.

Wolfgang quietly studied one of the shark teeth as he sat opposite the Rebels. Nonchalantly he then picked up his Glock handgun and released the bullet clip, using it to scratch his bald head which had begun to drip with perspiration.

Suddenly the speedboat hit a surprise wave and a small cascade of water flew across the open deck drenching everyone and every piece of equipment with warm seawater. Wolfgang just shook the water out of his eyes and laughed strangely. He then wiped his face and hopped up onto the metal platform.

"See? My delightful machine gun is waterproof! Waves, rain, a storm, nothing can destroy its firing mechanism!"

Travis just turned his head away bored. "Lucky you."

Then Travis saw it again.

Twenty yards behind the speedboat the distinct shape of a black dorsal fin could be seen trailing the speedboat's wake. The fin was immense in size, far larger than an ordinary Great White or Killer Whale. Without looking back he nudged Amber's shoulder.

Certain Wolfgang was distracted she spun towards Travis whispering, "What is it?" Her eyes widened at the stunning sight and she promptly elbowed Maddox.

Coolly Maddox peeked back and saw the black fin just before it slipped beneath the turquoise water. Calmly all three Treasure Rebels then looked towards their captor as if nothing had happened, but their minds were now working at a furious speed. It was obvious the same creature Travis had spotted in the ruins was now following the speedboat...and it was larger, and faster, than any underwater creature they knew of in the world.

As they puzzled over what type of species it could be, Amber spotted the gladiator helmet reflecting sunlight through one of the plastic tubs. Her thoughts drifted back to the ancient account of the shark-like creature the gladiator claimed to have killed. She couldn't help but wonder...what if the story was true...with no exaggerations?

Wolfgang grew tired of examining the machine gun and instead jumped down with bravado onto the deck. He then curtly grabbed the papers he had stolen from the *Wild Adventure* and handed the Australian flight manifest from the 1970's to Maddox.

"I was talking here with the Doctor earlier and he was surprised when I explained to him that the reports of the Rainforest Rogue's fateful plane crash were a little lacking."

Maddox simply dropped the paper back onto the deck at Wolfgang's feet.

"I'm not interested in the past. Neither are you baldy."

Wolfgang wasn't put off by Maddox's cold response. He reached down and read the old document from beginning to end, turning to Maddox quizzically once finished.

"Doctor Monette here was perplexed when I told him the flight manifest and police reports were wrong. They state only three men were on board, the Rogue, Tyson, and Creggs. But you and I Maddox know better... there were five men on board that plane instead of just three. Care to explain who those men were? They're both very important to the Rainforest Rogue's sad story."

Travis and Amber looked up in astonishment but Maddox's face remained unreadable.

The seconds went by and Wolfgang quietly snarled as Maddox stayed stubbornly quiet. The emaciated criminal then opened his mouth to speak but was stopped as his phone began ringing. The man by the wheel tossed him the smartphone.

"It's her again Boss."

With his bony fingers he tapped the screen and placed it to his ear.

"We're not at the dive site yet."

Tamla replied, "Trouble here. My father can't find his friend the archaeologist. And another passenger is missing as well. He's ordered the crew to search the yacht from top to bottom to find them."

"Is it possible your father knows the archaeologist is a thief?"

She shook her head and replied back confidently, "He's completely in the dark. If he doesn't know what I'm doing, there's no way he'd be smart enough to catch on to Renzo."

Wolfgang replied, "You think Renzo suspects someone is after the teeth?"

"That's what I'm afraid of. He has to know after he stole them at the auction last month he'd be targeted. Did you get a chance to look at the folder in the safe? That might tell us more about him."

He looked down and scooped the folder off the deck. "I will check it over now."

"How long till you reach the dive site? The sooner the better."

"Ten minutes."

"Can you really trust the Rebels to bring up the treasure?"

He looked up at the open sea. There wasn't a boat in sight.

"They have nowhere to go but bring the treasure back to me."

He ended the call then ripped open the folder's seal. Angrily he pulled out ten glossy colour photos and five other pages from a shipping order that were stapled together.

He quickly looked each photo over and barely studied the shipping order. He then gave the stack of papers to the Rebels saying, "It's nothing but pictures of a swamp in the jungle somewhere...and a shipping order for some scuba gear that looks half a century old. Mean something to you three?"

A sense of unease hit the Treasure Rebels as they looked at the glossy jungle pictures. But once they saw the shipping order, their unease turned to disbelief then alarm.

==

(*Moments Later – Blue Flower Yacht*)

Kozan anxiously looked at his luxurious pocket watch. "Hurry up and call your brother or those treasure hunters are dead!"

Renzo smiled and shook his head at Kozan. "I would not panic yet."

He then stuck his head outside the janitor closet to double check no-one was approaching. Certain the walkway along the rail was empty he closed the door again and confidently began dialling a number on his phone.

"My brother will not fear these people."

Kozan looked at the archaeologist puzzled, "Why so calm? These are professional criminals we're dealing with!"

Renzo smiled knowingly, "Don't be so fearful Mr. Kozan! My brother will be able to handle them."

"Who exactly is your brother anyway?"

Renzo finished dialling and looking up answered proudly, "Hector Bragard."

PART VI: SPINNING BLADES

The black speedboat slowed to a quiet stop near a small island. The small isle featured a six hundred foot long beach and a large eighty foot high hill covered in trees and green brush, while the top of the hill was flat and clear of any plant growth.

Wolfgang looked down at the water and barked up to the man at the wheel, "Water depth?"

"Shallow."

Wolfgang turned away from the turquoise water and with a wolfish wink he looked at the Rebels. "You three ready for your last dive?"

Warily Travis reached for the nearest dive tank but the cold barrel of a machine gun slapped down across his arm. Angrily he pushed the barrel away. "Enough games. I need my gear."

The crewman ignored Travis' comment and tossed the scuba tank to his bald leader.

Wolfgang explained gleefully, "I just want you three to dive down and back up. No need for any scuba equipment."

The Rebels were then released from the handcuffs and wearing only their black dive suits were prodded by the machine gun to the rail's edge. Nervously they scanned the water for any sign of the black shark fin.

Behind them Wolfgang taunted, "Remember. I have Dr. Monette. So return promptly."

Still tied to the rail Gunnar looked up at his daughter and said, 'I'll be fine Amber. I love you." She blew him a sad kiss then jumped in. A second later Travis leaped into the sea.

Left alone Maddox prepared to dive next but the gunman blocked him with the gun barrel, forcing him to turn and face Wolfgang.

"Hand me those funky shades Maddox. You can't see underwater with them anyway."

Maddox smiled back, "Actually I can."

He then jumped backwards into the sea before anyone could stop him.

With no equipment and no back-up all three Treasure Rebels dove down determined they would find a way to escape.

They reached the seafloor and swam ten feet apart hurriedly looking for anything that might resemble the old Nazi's "treasure." Within seconds they spotted it.

Three old shipping containers from the 1950's, one blue, red, and grey, were resting on the Aegean Seafloor. The paint had faded and each container had multiple spots where the metal sides had been bent out of shape.

They swam down to the nearest container, the blue one, and examined the large doors. The rusted handles were secured in place by a large chain with an old padlock. Despite heavy corrosion it still held firm.

They looked at each other and despite the dangerous situation they were in they couldn't help but smile.

They were certain they had found the "treasure" they had been searching for years to find.

They resurfaced a couple hundred feet from the speedboat, only their heads visible. Ignoring Wolfgang's shouts they quickly took some deep breaths and talked out of their enemies' earshot, thinking over every possible way of escape.

"If we climb to the top of the hill we can signal passing aircraft."

Travis shook his head at Amber's idea, "Even if we reach the island they'll just follow us ashore. I haven't seen a plane for hours either." He then looked back at Wolfgang, "Still it's better than treading water hoping the skinny rat doesn't tear us into pieces with his big gun."

Amber looked quickly back at Gunnar, "Wolfgang took the flare gun from me and stored it somewhere near the speedboat's console. The first chance my Dad gets he'll fire it."

Maddox replied, "Our best chance is to get Wolfgang's goons into the water then try to get into and control the boat before they realize what's happening."

Two hundred feet away Wolfgang fired his Glock handgun into the air in impatient anger.

Maddox continued, "You two keep talking, I'll get something to cut the chains."

He then swam back to the speedboat and stopped within thirty feet of the chrome rail, calling up to his enemy.

"There's something down there but it's chained. I need bolt cutters."

Wolfgang eyed Maddox suspiciously and looked in every direction. Nothing but empty Aegean Sea. Leering down he hesitantly tossed Maddox four large keys on a rusty key ring.

"Something my grandpa left me. Open it up."

Maddox caught the ring with one hand and dove back under out of sight. Moments later he resurfaced beside his two friends.

Full of nervous anticipation they each took a deep breath then dove back down to see what had been hiding in each container for over half a century.

They headed straight back to the blue container. Maddox placed one of the keys squarely into the cold steel of the padlock. The mechanism inside turned. As Maddox pulled the padlock clear and let it float away, Amber dragged the chains to the side while Travis grasped the shipping container's handles.

Even underwater the rusted hinges could be heard groaning as the door slowly opened...to reveal hundreds of gold bars. The Rebels quickly pulled out a dozen slabs to get a better look deeper into the container. There was nothing in the crate except more gold.

Maddox examined one of the bars and noticed a strange marking stamped on the centre. It was obvious to him that the gold had not come from Europe, but was gold that had been taken by Wolfgang and the Bounty Hunter decades ago from a jungle and melted into bars. The financial value of the gold was easily hundreds of millions of dollars.

The Rebels had no interest. They hurriedly replaced the gold and relocked the door. This wasn't the treasure they wanted.

==

Up above the turquoise waters Wolfgang and his men waited edgily for the Rebels to resurface.

Patience was not a virtue for Wolfgang. He sat down against the far rail and nervously stared across the water counting every second that went by. They had been underwater for a full minute.

He thought irritably: *They can hold their breath for a full hour for all I care. They can't go anywhere.*

But then a thought struck him.

But they are the Treasure Rebels.

Suddenly the quiet was broken by a distant rumble...from the sky.

Appearing above the island was a large grey transport helicopter. The helo slowly circled the speedboat then moved forward until it stopped and hovered seventy feet above the water.

The helicopter's cargo side door slid open and a monstrous sized man appeared. He sported an immense tangled black beard and arms covered in strange tattoos, while his eight nose rings reflected the afternoon sunlight.

Hector Bragard was one of the world's most dangerous black market thieves. Having been arrested in the Amazon Jungle after being outwitted by the Treasure Rebels, he had since used his wealth to bribe enough officials to have him released early from an obscure South American prison.

With the rotor wind snapping at his beard he glared down venomously at Wolfgang and wondered what the bald crook would do.

So this is the man who tried to steal from Renzo.

Apprehensively he shifted his eyes towards the unmanned machine gun. He then yelled at one of his men inside the chopper.

"Get me the rocket launcher."

In the speedboat below Wolfgang spoke to his crew without taking his eyes off Hector.

"Is the gun ready?"

The man by the wheel eyed the .50 caliber gun a couple feet above him.

"Just have to jump onto the platform and shoot."

"Excellent."

===

Maddox had just turned the key in the red container's padlock when he and the others paused to look up. The unmistakable rotor wash from a helicopter was visible on the surface. Could the Coast Guard have arrived? Their expressions filled with hope they swam for the surface.

===

A reinforced military case was placed next to Bragard's feet. As he unlocked the lid one of his men interrupted him, tapping him hysterically on the arm.

"You have...you have to see this!"

Bragard's famous temper flashed and he spun to viciously slap the man...but stopped when he saw the unbelievable sight below the helicopter.

A dark shape over thirty feet long was rapidly approaching Wolfgang's speedboat from beneath the water.

===

As they swam for the surface the Rebels stopped frozen in place, awed and horrified at the sight of the fast moving creature underwater. As the shark like beast drew closer and closer to the speedboat, Amber remembered the last line from the gladiator's written account: *"...the men still can't decide if it is a shark or monster."*

===

Wolfgang watched Bragard disappear back inside the helo. This was his chance. His eyes chillingly cold he gave the order.

"Blow the helicopter out of the-"

BOOM!

The speedboat was lifted up violently into the air as if hit by an underwater mine. The head and upper neck of an immense shark could be seen pushing the boat out of the water with brutal force. Wolfgang and his men were tossed thirty feet into the sky as the speedboat rotated end over end with Gunnar still handcuffed to the rail.

The shark was mostly dark coloured, and its large eyes appeared strangely shaped because of the odd patches of thick skin that acted like shields covering most of the eyeball. The creature's mouth was open with enormous strange teeth lining its upper jaw, while the bottom of the creature's mouth featured three spinning circular whorls that resembled giant circular blades. The largest blade in the centre was the size of a car tire, the two smaller ones each the size of a dinner plate. As the circular "plates" of jawbone spun the teeth cut through anything they touched, and every single tooth had the same similar shape as the teeth the Rebel's had recovered from the yacht safe.

The speedboat dropped with a wild splash back into the Aegean. But the third crewmember, the gunner, landed directly into the path of the thrashing shark's head. He disappeared inside the jaws before he could even scream.

The sharkish beast then began chewing mercilessly into the fiberglass frame, its rotating circular "blades" piercing through the boat's hull in seconds. The speedboat split in two and the side with Dr. Monette still attached sank below the surface.

Panicking the Rebels swam forward with everything they had. It didn't matter to them they were swimming *towards* the creature. They were determined to save Gunnar.

===

Bragard turned away from the shark attack below and hurriedly placed the unlocked rocket launcher case under a bench. He then pulled a silver lever next to the still open cargo door. Beneath the helicopter four thick cables began to lower towards the water while a large metal basket slid into position by the open doorway, secured to the helo by another set of smaller cables. Bragard turned and faced the two members of his gang standing uncertainly beside him in the cargo hold. Both men were dressed in full scuba gear...and looked petrified.

"You men know the plan. Attach the cables to one of the shipping containers below." He then pointed at the top of the small island. "We'll then drop it off atop the hill and repeat the process for the other two."

One of the men tepidly stepped to the edge and looked down at the terrible sight of the creature savagely chopping parts of the speedboat into tiny pieces.

"Shouldn't we wait for that...that...creature to go away?"

Bragard's savage eyes didn't blink and he replied, "The fish is preoccupied for now. You lose twenty grand of your paycheque if you don't step out this second."

Focusing on the money instead of common sense the two men climbed into the basket and Bragard hit the release button. The basket descended and the outline of the three shipping containers grew clearer as they approached the water.

===

The Rebels reached Gunnar and immediately began trying to break the rail and handcuff chain. Gunnar simply floated, unconscious. Amber hurriedly ripped a small sliver of chrome off one of the mangled seats and began trying to use it to pick the lock. But as hard as she tried the lock refused to spring open.

Maddox looked inside the shredded remains of the speedboat. Could any of their gear still be secured inside?

Nothing. It had all been tossed into the sea.

He looked down at the seafloor. Resting atop a clump of seaweed covered stones was one of the plastic containers...and one of their chainsaws sitting next to it.

He bolted for the chainsaw, his eyes briefly glimpsing the shark a hundred feet away, the spinning teeth now chopping the machine gun into small fragments. He ignored the freakish sight and kept swimming. He figured he could grab the chainsaw and return to cut Gunnar free in under half a minute.

But Gunnar didn't have that long. Travis could see the look of terror on Amber's face. A few more seconds and it might be too late.

Not today.

Travis looked for the weakest spot in the now twisted rail, and gripping the warped steel with both hands he began pushing with all his strength.

One second.

Two seconds.

It felt as if his wrists were about to *tear apart* but he responded by pushing even *harder*.

Finally the steel *snapped* like a broken twig and with one smooth motion Amber slid the handcuff off the rail. Travis then reached forward and grasping Gunnar in his huge arms swam rapidly for the surface.

==

Wolfgang viciously shook his face to clear his head. All he remembered was the speedboat flying in the air, the brief image of large shark teeth spinning into the boat, and the blue water as he landed. He blinked multiple times and examined his surroundings. Pieces of fiberglass and chrome wreckage lay scattered around him. Even part of the windscreen could be spotted reflecting light as it floated nearby.

No sign of the Treasure Rebels. Maybe they got eaten? He smiled at that thought. He then looked up and saw the helicopter with the wild looking bearded man was still there, now with two scuba divers descending towards the water in a large metal basket.

He reached for his sidearm but the gun was missing. He could spend a week searching the seafloor and still never find it.

He then spotted two of his crew a hundred yards away. Both men were waving their arms to get his attention. But where was the third crewmember? He didn't see the man anywhere. Then he realized...he couldn't see the shark either.

==

Dreading the worst Travis stepped out of the water carrying Gunnar followed closely behind by Amber. Carefully the former boxer laid the Doctor onto the white sand where Amber immediately began performing CPR.

Moments later Maddox surfaced, the specialized chainsaw in the sheath between his shoulder blades...and the flare gun and Amber's tablet in each hand.

Maddox tapped the computer screen and announced, "Signal strength back to normal. Whatever Wolfgang was using to jam the system it must have been chewed up by the shark. I'll try the Coast Gua-"

"Dad!"

Maddox looked up to see Gunnar turning to his side in agony and spitting up plenty of water. He was struggling to breath and coughed as if his lungs were barely working. His eyes met Amber's for a split second...and then he fainted again.

Amber went back to CPR more determined than ever while Maddox's call for help went through.

Just as the operator explained coldly to Maddox that help was currently unavailable, Gunnar sat up in pain and groggily awake.

As Amber hugged her father warmly Travis asked Maddox. "No luck?"

Maddox shook his head and tossed the tablet into Travis' chest. "Somethin' wrong man. Never heard a Coast Guard sound like that."

Just as he finished speaking he and Travis watched as the blue container with the gold was lifted out of the water and the large helo began moving up and towards the hilltop.

Their thoughts then went back to the shark attack.

"That's gotta be a Helicoprion shark!"

Amber looked up at Travis, "They went extinct eons ago."

Maddox replied, "The Helicoprion had only one circular whorl in its jaws. That wild shark has three...must be some sort of Helicoprion relative."

They looked back across the water. Wolfgang and his men were nowhere to be seen.

Travis adjusted the bloodied bandage across his arm and said, "They must be heading for the containers or they're already hiding somewhere on the beach."

Maddox instead watched the blue container slowly begin to lower towards the hilltop. Alarm in his voice he finally stated, "I've got to get the ancient Doctor's case before either of those nut jobs get it first."

He then looked at Amber still cradling Gunnar who was barely holding onto consciousness. He then handed Travis the flare gun saying, "You stay and guard them from Wolfgang. I'll get the case."

Travis checked the flare gun. The flare was still loaded and dry inside.

"Copy that."

Maddox then stepped into the water, the chainsaw in the sheath behind his back his only weapon. Stopping he looked back at his friends. Travis simply nodded his head while Amber called out, "Save it before Wolfgang gets it."

Maddox turned back and dove into the Aegean out of sight.

As Amber monitored her father Travis took the tablet and tried five different emergency services in Greece. Every operator told him the same thing: call the Coast Guard. Resisting the urge to violently toss the tablet into the sea in frustration he instead closed his eyes to concentrate and said, "Can you think of anyone we know who owns a boat or plane worth calling?" She shook her head dejectedly. "No. The only one is Peterson the dock keeper in Kefalonia. But it would take him days to sail here."

Travis kept his eyes closed thinking. Time was everything. They had to get Gunnar off the island as fast as possible to stabilize him...and before Bragard or Wolfgang could hunt them down.

Suddenly his eyes opened, smiling as if he had just won the heavyweight title. "Got it! I know the person to call!"

She looked up expectantly while he quickly dialled the number into the tablet.

"Who?"

===

Ten seconds later a smartphone resting atop a pile of books began ringing on one of Crete's eastern beaches. An attractive young woman set down her camera, tapped the phone's large screen, and lifted it to her ear.

"This is Victoria Desmond."

PART VII: ENEMIES EVERYWHERE

(Ten Minutes Later – Eastern Crete – Aircraft Hangar)

Victoria's purple jeep roared to a stop outside one of Crete's largest aircraft hangars. She jumped onto the warm tarmac and rushed through the open hangar doors. She turned to the left and stopped in front of a white and red trim single engine turboprop airplane, the fastest of its kind on the island.

"I need your help!"

Wearing blue overalls and a white hat that featured the logo of Greece's national soccer team, Clint Desmond stepped out from underneath the aircraft smiling knowingly.

"You're always looking for a favour, sis! I'm busy today. Four clients."

She wouldn't take no from her brother and explained, "I just received an emergency call from Travis Jagson. They need our help on one of those small isolated islands far east of here. Clint, it's an emergency!"

He tossed the wrench he had been carrying roughly into the tool kit at his feet, crossing his grease covered arms. "*Forget* them. That Maddox deserves nothing from you."

"Clint it- "

"He walked away from you without a word face to face. No-one treats my sister that way."

"It's Amber's father. He needs to be taken to a hospital. He'll probably die without us."

Clint wavered a little. He had never met Dr. Monette but had heard of the man's life saving medical work.

"Call the Coast Guard."

"They can't get through."

"What does that mean?"

She smiled at her brother. "That's the other favour."

He unfolded his arms, annoyed but resigned now that he would help her. "What would that *other favour* be?"

She pulled out her smartphone and replied, "Does your girlfriend Mila still work at the Coast Guard?"

==

Maddox swam close to the seafloor warily watching for any sign of the creature. So far all he had seen was some floating wreckage and the chewed remnants of the machine gun sitting in the silt. Carefully he kicked upward to take a breath, making certain that only his head broke the surface. Afraid the hot sunlight might reflect off his copper coloured shades and give away his position he took them off as well.

He filled his lungs with the deepest breath he could take, and looking up he spotted the outline of the helicopter still sitting atop the hill. Good.

He slipped back into the turquoise depths and replaced the sunglasses across his face, thankful the spring hinges kept the unusual sunglasses attached to his face while he swam. He thought back to the stunned look on Wolfgang's face when he had said he could see underwater wearing the shades. But then again, that was one of the reasons the sunglasses were priceless. They had been *designed* in part for diving.

He reached the bottom and kept moving forward until the two containers came back into view. He paused at the sight.

The grey container was still locked and chained while Wolfgang and his two men were using rocks they had picked up off the seafloor to try and smash open the red container's padlock. After a dozen hits the padlock finally broke and the criminals greedily swam inside.

Maddox carefully swam around the red container until he stopped in front of the final container's door. Thankfully the grey container had been placed a dozen feet behind the red one.

He pulled the discoloured key chain out of a leg pocket and slid one of the rusted keys into the padlock. It clicked free of the chains and floated down. As he grasped the chains a strange sound reverberated through the water from above. Looking up he could see the surface was once again agitated and a large shadow was hovering above the water. Bragard's helicopter was back.

He turned back to the container and pulled the chains away. His heart suddenly pounding in anticipation he grasped the handles and began unlocking the hinges...then froze as the broad side of a large jungle machete slapped down across his arm!

Maddox released the handles and the hinges slid back into place as Wolfgang clutching a machete moved closer. Maddox guessed the machete must have come from the red container. He then looked up and noticed the two other thieves were standing atop the red container glaring down at him...also holding similar blades.

Maddox slowly began swimming backward...just as he spotted the shark-like creature swim past the two containers only a couple feet behind Wolfgang's back. Instinctively Maddox dove around the edge of the grey container. Wolfgang didn't see the hideous shark but he saw the large shadow it cast and instantly dove for cover as well.

The two thieves panicked and instead swam for the surface as fast as they could. Fatal mistake. With Maddox and Wolfgang out of sight the shark's strange eyes focused on the motion of the two men kicking, and with a vicious snap of its immense tail it reversed course. The men were almost at the surface when the creature's strange jaws reached them.

==

Fifty feet above the water Bragard's two divers carefully stepped back into the metal basket. Bragard hit the switch and the basket slowly moved towards the blue water below.

"Look at that!"

The other diver followed his friend's pointed arm. Wolfgang's two men could be seen lifting their arms out of the water and swimming as fast as they could for land. Then suddenly the water beneath them turned into a frothing mess of bubbles and they vanished from sight. A moment later the turquoise water changed to a deep red colour.

Bragard's divers simply watched in quiet horror until...

The creature shot out of the water like a rocket spiralling and twisting thirty feet into the warm air...its spinning teeth missing the basket by mere inches!

The men leaped in fright and the basket tipped crazily. Screaming both men almost fell over the side and barely held on. The shark hit the sea below with a wild splash leaving a trail of water flying upwards that drenched both divers and the basket. Terrified they somehow regained their wits and calmed down enough to keep the basket steady. Yelling hoarsely they signalled Bragard to pull them up.

Bragard complied and smacked the switch.

Climbing frantically into the cargo bay moments later one of the divers ripped off his mask and glared at Bragard. It was unthinkable that any of them would challenge their leader who was a known killer, but after seeing the monster below the diver suddenly had lost all fear of the bearded monster who had hired him.

"I ain't diving with that beast from a horror movie right below us!"

Bragard simply waved his hand annoyed as if the man had nothing to worry about and handed over the machine gun strapped to his thigh.

"Fill the fish with lead!"

==

Maddox and Wolfgang slowly looked up to where the two men had last been seen. There was nothing but a cloud of blood. Wolfgang gripped the handle of the machete even tighter and pressed his back up against the container door in fright looking frantically for the shark. While the sight of the blood made Maddox's stomach sick, he forced himself to swim away from Wolfgang and onto the red container roof.

Once atop the corroded red steel he could see the Helicoprion "cousin" was now circling the two containers...and every second drawing closer. Maddox then looked up and could see Bragard's chopper was still hovering above and that four cables had been dropped into the water, the metal rings floating a couple feet below the surface.

He then watched as the shark looped closer. He drew the chainsaw with his finger on the red trigger. The shark was now only forty feet away.

The thought then passed through his mind about swimming into the open red container to hide. He gave up on that idea quickly. What if the shark spotted him and followed him inside?

Ping! Ping! Smack!

Bullets fired from the helicopter above tore through the water peppering the seafloor and the red container roof. One bullet ricocheted off the chainsaw frame then created a spark as it hit the reinforced metal chain. In one smooth motion Maddox swam off the roof towards the seafloor as the bullets continued to splatter the red container and pierce through the open water in every direction. He hoped the creature hadn't spotted him.

A bullet creased Wolfgang's scalp leaving a permanent scar if he survived the day. Realizing Bragard was trying to shoot the shark from above he spun around to the other side of the grey container out of the shooter's line of fire.

The shark *had* seen Maddox and Wolfgang move and was closing in. But as it got close three bullets tore into the beast's extremely thick outer skin and more agitated than seriously wounded it turned irritably back and disappeared in the opposite direction.

==

Travis paced back and forth in alarm, "Bragard's goons are shooting up the water like maniacs! I've gotta go in to back Maddox up!"

He took ten steps towards the water before he stopped to look back at Amber and her father. Her face was pale white with distress while the barely conscious doctor rested in her arms, his gaunt face mumbling unintelligibly.

Travis spit angrily into the sand in frustration...he simply couldn't leave them behind on the island in case any of their enemies suddenly re-appeared. He walked away from the water and stood with his back to a large tree trunk and crossed his arms, the flare gun ready, keeping watch.

===

"It's swimming away! You must have hit it very good!"

The other diver released the trigger and the machine gun stopped firing.

"You sure you see it?"

His equally frightened associate replaced the binoculars tight against his eyes. The dark form of the strange shark could be clearly seen moving to the right towards the open sea. Satisfied he nodded back then turning to look into the cargo hold he yelled as loud as he could over the engine roar.

"It's leaving the area! We'll be able to dive safely in-"

The hairy Bragard curtly replied, "You only need five seconds to attach the cables."

Then without waiting for a response he hit the switch and the metal basket began descending again.

===

Maddox broke the surface and took a deep breath, dropping back into the Aegean before Bragard or his men could spot him. He headed straight for the grey container. This was his chance. The shark was gone at least for now. Wolfgang was nowhere to be seen so that meant he was probably raiding the red container again.

He grasped the grey door handles. This was it. Over two years of searching for this "treasure" that mattered more to him and his friends than any gold.

He pushed the handles to the edge, the hinges turned, and the door slowly groaned open allowing sunlight through the water to burst inside. Visible were three wooden crates filled with ancient roman weapons, while secured to the left wall was the missing half of the Roman mosaic from the ruins armoury, and resting at the very back of the container was a metal storage cabinet from the 1950's.

The mosaic was beautiful to look at, depicting a gladiator in the sea impaling what appeared to be a giant Helicoprion shark with a green coloured sword.

The crates were filled with gladiator shields, swords, helmets, spears, and even leg greaves. The decades underwater had led to every weapon severely rusting...except one. Reflecting the sunlight was a special looking blade wrapped in plastic for preservation. Maddox leaned into the crate and pulled out the "mythical" ancient sword the gladiator had used to kill the monstrous shark eighteen hundred years earlier.

The sword's handle was made of strong dark wood and the long blade had been crafted in the shape of a gladius. A marvel of blacksmithing, what Maddox guessed was purple gemstone had somehow been woven into the steel of the blade in the shape of multiple spiders, while gold trim was laced near the sides of the blade. Without wasting another second he placed the ancient blade still wrapped in plastic alongside the chainsaw behind his back.

With his heart beating in wild expectation he rapidly moved past the crates and mosaic towards the steel cabinet.

He found what he was looking for in the first drawer.

A wooden box roughly the size of a hardback book with the words etched into the front: *Rimor Markos.*

He hurriedly placed the treasured box in a pocket by his lower back.

Suddenly he noticed the shadows shift inside and he looked back to see Wolfgang's ugly maniacal face laughing as he closed the container door and locked Maddox inside!

Maddox remained calm refusing to panic. This wasn't the first time he had been seemingly trapped. He turned in the now dark water and felt the warm steel of the container wall. He then pulled the chainsaw out of the sheath behind his back and confidently pushed the red trigger.

Nothing happened.

The chain refused to spin to life.

He quickly remembered the shooter from above and the bullet ricocheting off the frame and chain. The bullet must have broken the internal engine.

He then pushed the black switch. No response. The heat function was also damaged.

With growing dread he tried sliding the chainsaw across the metal in hopes of cutting through. Without the power of the spinning chain the serrated bits just dug into the metal and became stuck.

Underwater and in the dark, he was now literally trapped.

===

Bragard's two divers cautiously entered the water, closed the red container door and went to work securing the cables. But in seconds they realized three of the four metal rings on the roof had corroded away. Anxious to already be out of the water they eyed the grey container. Even from thirty feet away they could easily see all four metal rings were visible on the grey roof.

Moments later Maddox heard the eerie footsteps above his head as Bragard's men secured the cables to the grey container roof. He then heard the metal creak above as the divers left. He only had seconds to get out before the helicopter pulled away.

He gave up on the chainsaw and left it wedged in the steel. Instead he lifted the gladiator sword from behind his back and ripped the plastic away while swimming forward to the door.

The sword felt brand new. But would it still be sharp?

There was no handle to open the door from the inside. So he began sawing into the door hinges while hoping Wolfgang hadn't replaced the chains around the handle outside.

Suddenly the container rocked forward then back as it was lifted out of the silt. He had only moments before the container became airborne.

Snap!

The sharp blade sliced completely through the first rusted hinge. He quickly sawed into the second one.

Snap!

It was now gone as well and he re-sheathed the sword. Then steadying himself he pushed against the door with both hands. But the water pressure was too strong to push it open from the inside.

A moment later the container swayed as it broke free of the Aegean. He fell to one knee because of the motion as the water began rushing out through the cuts and cracks in the steel frame.

Jumping forward he *rammed* the door as hard as possible with his shoulder. The door broke open a couple feet and most of the water that remained inside poured out.

He then pushed the door fully open and looked down, coughing as he breathed in the sea air. The Aegean was twenty feet below. No problem for him.

He took a step back then jumped clear of the container...only to have Wolfgang reach down from above and grab him with one hand in mid-air! Stunned he was pulled up and roughly thrown onto the metal roof at Wolfgang's feet.

Maddox jumped up wondering why Wolfgang had climbed onto the container. He then noticed far below a dark shadow moving in the water below the helicopter. No wonder Wolfgang had climbed aboard instead of staying underwater. The monstrous shark had returned.

As the container continued to slowly move upwards Maddox spun and faced his old enemy.

Still holding the machete Wolfgang rubbed the saltwater out of his goatee and said, "So we finally found my grandfather's treasure!" He then pointed with the weapon towards the gladiator sword behind Maddox's back. "Is that what you and the other two have been after all these years?"

Before Maddox could reply Wolfgang attacked swinging the machete wildly. Maddox easily ducked but Wolfgang followed with a vicious punch that connected directly into Maddox's chest. He dropped to his knees stunned at the pain then rolled to the side just in time to avoid another strike from the jungle blade.

He then reached back and drew the famous gladiator sword, blocking another swing from Wolfgang. The bare steel of the machete blade met the ancient steel of Rome. Crackling sparks sizzled in the air where the two weapons met.

Maddox jumped to his feet and blocked another strike then brought the sword down across Wolfgang's side. Wolfgang screeched as the sword cut across the length of his arm.

Maddox followed with a hard right cross aimed at Wolfgang's head. But the sociopath avoided the punch and grabbed Maddox's arm, throwing the treasure hunter behind him with a wild yell, the expression in his criminal eyes even wilder. Maddox landed hard on his back and Dr. Markos' box slid out of the back pocket and tumbled towards the edge. Scrambling Maddox scooped up the treasure and replaced it just as Wolfgang drew close again swinging the machete violently. He avoided every slice but Wolfgang was close to simply overpowering him.

Looking down from the helicopter above Bragard was stunned to see Maddox Tarver again. But he was even more stunned to see the fabled sword in Maddox's hand. The priceless ancient weapon was *his* main reason for searching for the gladiator helmet in the Amazon and now the old treasure filled shipping containers. As much as he hated the leader of the Treasure Rebels, Bragard couldn't risk Maddox losing to Wolfgang. If Maddox was killed or was thrown off the container the sword might be lost forever.

Agitated to the point of almost hysteria he frantically turned to his men. "Hold the helicopter still! I can't risk the one in the sunglasses falling back into the water. And bring the container up higher!"

One of the men replied, "Mr. Bragard that's as high as the winch will take it."

"I see."

Having lost his reason to greed and with a grunt of brutal determination he smacked the switch then hopped into the metal basket as it began descending. When the basket was within a dozen feet of the grey container he jumped clear.

The container rattled as Bragard's t six foot nine, two hundred and seventy pound frame landed heavily onto the roof feet first. He reached for his machine gun but Wolfgang leaped and tackled him. The machete and the machine gun both clattered to the roof in the struggle and soon both men were fighting using only punches, kicks, and attempted choke holds.

Wolfgang grasped Bragard's arm in a judo lock and with effort he threw Bragard over his shoulder. The bearded criminal landed *hard* onto his back, the entire container now *shuddering* at the fierce impact.

Maddox barely watched. Instead he looked up at the helicopter then down at the water, then at the island in the distance. He figured his options were simple: stay atop the container and likely be killed by Bragard, Wolfgang, or Bragard's trigger happy gunmen, or jump and hopefully reach the beach before the shark locked onto him.

Better to face the predator below which *might* kill him, instead of facing the human predators who would kill him for *certain*.

He put the sword back in the scabbard behind his head and made sure the wooden case was secure. He then stepped to the edge and readied himself. He estimated the jump was about fifty feet. But the helo had moved away from the shallow water so a jump from this height would be safe.

He looked back at his enemies fighting then back at the water. The shark had suddenly circled back and was directly below. Maddox decided he would wait as long as he could till the shark had turned away.

The roof suddenly groaned under the weight of the three men and the four corroded bolts the cables were attached to began to bend under the stress...and then two *snapped* in half.

The container dropped fifteen feet then shook crazily as the two remaining cables stretched dangerously under the weight. Maddox was thrown forward into empty space until he reached back as he was falling and grabbed the edge of the roof with one hand.

Wolfgang was thrown violently onto his face while Bragard crashed over the side, clutching the nearest cable with both of his beefy hands to keep from falling. With only one cable now at each end the container continued to swing wildly back and forth in the open air.

His entire body dangling over the water Maddox held on and looked down...to see the enormous shark jumping out of the water directly towards the container!

The shark's head reached the grey steel bottom and the three spinning sets of horrible jagged teeth sliced into the rusted metal leaving a massive ten foot long gash. The already weakened metal spilt the rest of the way and the crates of ancient gladiator weapons began spilling out towards the Aegean below along with the metal cabinet.

The force of the shark's jaws smashing upwards into the steel fiercely rocked the entire container...and Maddox and Bragard were sent flying towards the water.

The massive shark landed back into the Aegean with a powerful splash, followed by Bragard who fell in headfirst, then the cabinet, then Maddox. Moments later the rotted crates hit the water's surface and began sinking from view.

As the container shook crazily Wolfgang lay flat across the roof and desperately held on while the pilot did his best to steady the helicopter which was tipping to one side. Bragard's men held on inside the cargo bay and barely avoided being thrown outside. But plenty of supplies including the rocket launcher slid across the cargo bay and out through the open door.

Maddox blinked to clear his vision ten feet below the water surface, his eyes catching dozens of rusted swords and pieces of Roman armour floating down through the water around him. He then spotted the red container a hundred feet ahead. The shark was nowhere to be seen. Without hesitation he kicked towards the island. But was wrenched back as Bragard's beefy tattooed arms wrapped around his neck from behind!

Maddox tried to break free but Bragard was too strong. He started coughing out what oxygen remained in his lungs and he feared the last thing he would ever see was Bragard's bizarre tattoos.

Still holding tightly Hector then let go with one arm and pulled the gladiator sword out of the scabbard behind Maddox's head. Afraid his attacker might now try to stab him, Maddox turned to break free but instead of escaping ended up now facing his cruel adversary face to face.

All Maddox could see was a mass of black hair floating in the water...Bragard's immense beard. He grabbed the beard with both hands and yanked to the right as hard as he could.

The hairy killer gurgled in painful agony and Maddox was free. Bragard madly swung the sword as Maddox escaped but the underwater resistance slowed the blade down and Maddox easily avoided it, spinning away.

Bragard gave chase as Maddox swam inches out of his grasp. Then Maddox spotted a Roman shield floating down, bent out of shape and rusted almost beyond recognition. He reached out anyway and grabbed the ancient metal in both hands, rotating back and smashing it directly into Bragard's face.

Bragard shook his head to clear away the pain then slashed at Maddox who raised the deteriorated shield in defense. The Roman shield barely deflected the sword. Bragard then pulled back and stabbed forward. The sharp blade pierced straight through the metal, the purple and gold blade missing Maddox's side by inches. With the sword now stuck Maddox spun the shield which twisted Bragard's arm.

The bearded criminal yanked the sword free but just as he did so the giant shark reappeared swimming directly between the two men fighting. Maddox let go of the shield and kicked backwards while Bragard stared at the strange looking creature in disbelief.

The shark continued to swim past until Bragard lost his nerve and lunged at the shark trying to stab it through the side. The creature instinctively curled away and the nine foot high tail slapped against Bragard's head.

The force of the blow almost cracked Bragard's skull and the gladiator sword floated out of his grasp and settled blade first into the dark mud. Now unconscious he couldn't move as the shark closed in and ended his evil life with one ferocious bite.

Maddox instead swam as fast as he possibly could for the last container. He opened the red door a couple feet and wriggled inside. What little sunlight there was shining through the open door revealed crates full of old excavation equipment, drills, and machetes.

Unbelievably also sitting in the centre was the partial preserved skeleton of an ancient shark. The dim light revealed the head featured a giant circular whorl, while dozens of the shark's teeth were missing. A giant Helicoprion, no doubt the same one the gladiator had killed centuries ago and written about.

Maddox closed the door and swam into the now fully dark interior.

How long did he need to wait for the shark to leave? More importantly, how much longer could he hold his breath?

Counting the seconds he spun his head to look back at the container door...just as the serrated whirling teeth began chewing through the steel door towards him!

==

High above the water Wolfgang watched below at what he correctly presumed was Maddox swimming towards the container, then the mighty shape of the shark following behind. Wolfgang then spotted the rocket launcher box resting inside the metal basket and he smiled wickedly.

With a weird yell he leaped off the container and grabbed onto the basket, pulling himself inside. Steadying himself he then opened the box and prepared the deadly launcher.

==

Maddox pressed his back against the far corner as the giant shark tore inside the container, slicing through the crates, equipment, and old bones. The creature suddenly became disoriented and closed its jaws as it reached the end, smashing into the wall with its black nose. The metal shrieked and the welds tore free leaving a two foot gap in the very top of the back wall.

He tried to swim past the creature towards the sawed open door. But he immediately froze as he was pushed back by the immense force of the shark's colossal tail that was thrashing violently back and forth. That left only one option.

He spun back and grasped the top of the shark's nose with both hands and propelled himself forward and up towards freedom. His head, arms, and chest shot through the two foot gap at the top and out into the clear water...but the creature unexpectedly pulled back and the metal sheet closed...pinning Maddox at the stomach! He wriggled and struggled to pull himself clear but the wooden case secured to his lower back made it impossible to squeeze through. He reached back and with great strain pulled the case free and flung it away into open water.

Screaming with determination he then strained to pull his legs clear just as he felt the spinning teeth begin to cut into the soles of his feet from below.

===

Wolfgang lifted the now ready rocket launcher onto his shoulder. He set the sights and snarled with dark determination.

"Goodbye Maddox."

He then pressed the trigger and the rocket blasted towards the container.

==

(Island Beach)

Travis and Amber watched in horror as they spotted the rocket slicing through the air then disappear from view as it entered the water.

Boom!

An eruption of water, blood, shark innards, bones, and scraps of metal flew into the sky.

"Maddox!!"

Still kneeling by her father Amber then looked away from the scene of carnage and up at Travis.

"Do you see him?"

Travis kept staring at the blood stained water.

He finally replied after a long ten seconds.

"No."

The horrible silence was broken as a loud horn echoed from high above the trees.

Two Coast Guard helicopters were rapidly flying towards Bragard's helo.

Then Amber spotted a fast approaching single engine plane further in the distance.

"Victoria's here."

==

The Coast Guard choppers took up aggressive flight positions in front and in back of Bragard's helicopter.

Now certain Bragard was dead the three men inside followed the Coast Guard's directions and landed atop the island, after first setting down what remained of the grey container and Wolfgang in the basket. All three of Bragard's men then raised their arms in surrender while Wolfgang was forced onto the hard ground at gunpoint. The bald sociopath then felt the chilled steel of handcuffs tighten around his wrists once again.

===

Clint Desmond smoothly landed the small aircraft onto the beach, rolling to a stop a hundred feet from Amber and Travis, the flare gun still smoking in Travis' hand after having been fired a minute before.

Gunnar was immediately loaded and secured behind the pilot and co-pilot seats.

Travis and Amber then quickly hugged Victoria and thanked her. Clint instead didn't move from his seat, only nodding his head hello.

Victoria then asked bluntly, "Where's Maddox?"

Travis couldn't bring himself to explain, "He's...uh scuba diving."

She then leaned into the plane and pulled out a large orange box.

"Here's the inflatable raft you asked for! It's small but durable. Do you need anything else?"

Travis pointed up at the top of the hill. "We got the Coast Guard now to help us."

She nodded her head then looked at Amber while pointing to the co-pilot's chair. "You should go! I can stay."

Amber didn't respond but instead stepped into the plane and knelt beside her father. Over the engine noise she stated, "Victoria will stay with Travis."

Gunnar turned to look at her, his face pale but his eyes now clear and very strong.

"Is Maddox okay?"

"Maddox is still in the water. But the Coast Guard is here. They'll help Maddox if needed."

"But what if Maddox needs help before then?"

She looked out at the water, then hugged her Dad holding back tears, "See you in Crete."

"See you in Crete."

She then quickly closed the door and stepped away from the plane.

Understanding Amber was staying, Victoria waved goodbye, but paused before stepping back inside the aircraft.

"Tell Maddox..." She couldn't find the words.

Travis understood. "I'll tell him."

Her heart heavy she stepped back into the cockpit as Travis and Amber ran to the water's edge. In seconds the plane was airborne and headed for Crete's finest hospital, while Travis and Amber inflated the raft and rowed out to find their friend.

As the island began to grow smaller in the distance Victoria stated flatly, "We'll wait for them at the hospital."

"Can't. There's no way I can leave the plane there for hours. We've got to head back to the hangar once we drop the doctor off. You're also forgetting your car. It'll be towed at the hangar if you don't pick it up."

She grinned, "Okay. I'll get the car and drive back to see Maddox."

==

Travis and Amber rowed out directly to where they had seen the explosion. Without another word they both leaped into the water in different directions not sure what they would find below.

A minute later Amber emerged out of the water and placed one hand atop the raft. "I can't find Maddox!" She looked up. Travis still hadn't resurfaced.

A moment of panic set in. Had something happened to Travis too?

Just then he broke the surface carrying their unconscious friend yelling, "Get him in!'

She leaped into the raft and helped Travis lift Maddox out of the water.

Without hesitation she began CPR while Travis watched in fear. Maddox's dive suit was torn, his feet were bleeding, and both legs sported nasty dark red bruises.

Amber moved aside and Travis replaced her, instead doing only chest compressions. The seconds went by and Maddox remained motionless.

Travis refused to stop.

A horrific and long minute later...Maddox sprang back to life.

He coughed up three mouthfuls of water then rubbed his stinging eyes beneath the sunglasses mumbling, "Where's Gunnar?"

"Dad's safely on his way to the hospital."

"Wolfgang?"

"Coast Guard finally came."

Maddox just nodded and said, "The shark was right inside the container with me. I was swimmin' away...then everything went boom."

Travis motioned towards a large piece of burnt steel floating nearby, "Wolfgang blew up the container with a rocket launcher."

Maddox grinned faintly, the swagger coming back. "Good thing the treasure wasn't inside."

"You're sure?"

"Tossed it clear before the rocket hit."

Amber suddenly pointed at something floating in the water. "There it is!" Before Travis or Maddox could say anything she had jumped into the blue water...returning moments later with the old wooden box tucked under one arm.

"Spotted it floating away on the surface! I couldn't miss seeing the word Markos printed on the front!"

They just sat and stared at the "treasure" box, somewhat stunned they finally had it. The reason Maddox had asked Travis and Amber to join him and become treasure hunters. Treasure more important than any gold, silver, or fame.

Maddox lifted the old key ring out of the dive suit pocket and opened the mysterious old box with the fourth and final key. Sunlight poured inside the box revealing five papyrus pages covered with words handwritten in Latin, while resting beside the papyrus was a large glass vial filled with a bluish coloured liquid. In the bottom of the box were ancient measuring and medical instruments.

Travis lifted the vial out of the box and stared at the liquid lost in thought, the ancient glass reflecting the afternoon sunlight off his face. Maddox instead took the papers and handed them to Amber. She quickly looked over each page, able to read and translate Latin faster than they could.

"Everything your Dad needs?"

She smiled, "Everything."

===

(Later that evening – Crete Hospital)

Victoria stepped into the large hospital waiting room before the help desk which was staffed by two tired looking nurses. She explained she was a friend of the Monette family and wished to visit if possible.

The head nurse lifted a clipboard off the desk and studying it closely replied, "Sorry dear, Dr. Gunner Monette left a half hour ago."

"What! He nearly died earlier today! Where did he go?"

The nurse took off her glasses and sighed explaining, "We tried to keep him overnight. His daught-"

"Yes, Amber Monette."

"Yes, Miss Monette and those two wild friends of hers were carrying some sort of box...and when Dr. Gunnar saw what was inside he...well, he literally leaped out of bed and insisted he be allowed to leave. The poor man, he practically ran out of the building with them yelling to us he had life-saving work to do."

Victoria stepped back slightly stunned then replied, "Did they leave a message?"

The nurse smiled, "All three told me to tell you they appreciate what you did for the doctor. The one with the scars even said they'll be sending you some money."

"The one with the scars?"

"Uh huh, the one with the blond hair. Took me forever to get him to take those sunglasses off in here."

PART VIII: TREASURE UNLIKE ANY OTHER

(One Day Later – Western Crete Airport)

Renzo pulled the brim of his archaeologist hat low over his eyes. Standing in line at the checkout he could see the passenger plane through the large windows outside. He just had to get his ticket stamped, board the plane, and he would be forever free of Greece...and its police.

He looked up and could see none of the people in line closest to him were passengers from Megalos' yacht.

Good. No-one to identify me.

Suddenly the crowd quieted and all conversations stopped as two security guards appeared from behind the check-out desk. Moving quickly they approached someone near the front of the line out of Renzo's line of sight.

A second later the horrible whine of Tamla shrieking filled the room as the young woman kicked one of the security guards and ran for the parking lot doors as fast as her scrawny legs would carry her. She never came close, completely disappearing underneath six more guards who tackled her swiftly to the carpet. Still wailing she was carried to one of the interview rooms behind the check-out desk where three Interpol agents were waiting patiently for her with an arrest warrant.

Everyone in the airport cheered. Keeping his head down Renzo smiled.

Good. The skinny witch deserves a jail cell.

But unexpectedly the cheers died down. Renzo looked up as to why.

Three more security guards had appeared by the line...and they had him surrounded.

One leaned forward and snapped a pair of steel handcuffs across his chubby wrists.

"Please come with us...Mr. Bragard."

==

(Two Days Later – Crete Police Headquarters)

Captain Megalos nervously stepped into the Chief of Police's large oak panelled office.

Megalos had aged a couple years in the past three days. His daughter was being held in prison without bail facing over ten international criminal charges. His beautiful ship was tied up in dry-dock being combed over by the police. And the stolen safe had never been returned, despite his promise to the passengers.

He sat down and the Chief of Police, a fifty-something man with a large white-grey moustache named Giorgos, spoke.

"How're you feelin' Megalos?"

He felt like a failure. As a father. And as a captain. But all he did was smile weakly and reply, "Just bumpy seas as they say, Chief."

"My detectives inform me your daughter has been involved in a lot of black market dealings. Much of it across Europe. If it's any consolation we know you've had nothing to do with those activities."

Megalos shifted in his chair a little. "What will happen to her?"

"She'll likely end up in a French or British jail for many, many, years."

"What of the man she was working with? This Wolfgang fellow I hear about on the news?"

"He was caught months ago in the Congo jungle. He's been involved in everything from forgery, international theft, murder, and fraud. He was tucked away in prison for the next fifty years until he broke out about two weeks ago. Your daughter was one of the ones who funded his escape."

"Is my daughter facing life in prison?"

"Unlikely. But the sentence will be a long one. She'll spend most of her adult life behind bars."

The Chief then opened a worn police file and handed Megalos a large black and white photo continuing, "It also appears that she was working with one of our own men here in the Coast Guard. After the robbery aboard your yacht she made multiple calls to his number, where he then misled officials here and delayed our response in helping the treasure hunters. Thankfully another staffer...a Mila Robson, discovered what was going on in the office and exposed the rat in time."

Megalos shook his head, "Can't identify him. Never seen him on my yacht or with Tamla."

Giorgos took the photo and tossed it back inside the worn file. "It's all right, we've rounded up the entire group, all of Wolfgang's men and the crew that funded and broke him out of the jungle prison." He then tossed the file angrily onto a nearby table with disgust, "They'll all rot in jail as long as Wolfgang will...along with Renzo."

"My friend Renzo? What could he possibly have to do with the robbery?"

"Your friend Renzo isn't just an archaeologist. He's also a world class electrical engineer and pro thief. He's worked with his recently deceased brother Hector for years. He designed a special type of scuba gear for his brother to use that can withstand high pulses of electricity underwater and can also be worn inside of caves. A bit of a nutcase for history, he even designed the suits to look like ones built over half a century ago. The only flaw in the design was that every suit had to be attached to a long cable when underwater...something about providing power for the underwater tools."

Giorgos then turned the old computer monitor on his desk around so the screen showing Renzo's mug shot faced Megalos. "He stole the shark teeth which apparently contained evidence where the shipping containers were sitting on the seafloor. It appears the Bragard brothers and Wolfgang's crew along with your daughter have been searching for those crates for a long time."

"The two men who stole the safe on my ship, which side were they on?"

"Neither. They were independent. They intended to steal the teeth themselves at an auction before Renzo surprised them and stole the teeth first. They tracked Renzo to your yacht."

"Did my daughter know about Renzo?"

"Yes, and about the robbery. She apparently planned to search the safe and copy whatever details were in the folder and on the teeth and relay the information to Wolfgang. But when Mr. Baris and Mr. Talib stole the safe in the middle of the day everyone's plans changed. And instead of one group winning, they're all going to jail. Well, the ones that didn't get eaten."

"I don't believe that part. I've been sailing for almost half a century, gave up believing in sea monsters as a teenager."

Giorgos typed a few keys on the keyboard and a vivid image of the famous Helicoprion shark filled the screen.

"Not a monster Megalos. There wasn't much of it left after the explosion, but the experts tell me they believe it was some sort of relative of the ancient Helicoprion ratfish. Apparently a similar...*shark* was spotted by the Romans long ago, but no-one believed the story till now."

Giorgos then cleared his throat and continued, "As if that wasn't enough, another new species of shark was discovered in the underwater ruins. Most sharks in these waters aren't predatory towards people. But these "Greek Gladiator Sharks" are man-eaters for sure."

The Chief then folded his hands under his chin and looked straight at Megalos with harsh eyes.

"You'll be asked to testify at the different trials, and the *Blue Flower* is landlocked indefinitely as we complete a full inquiry. Any questions?"

"None."

Giorgos turned the screen back saying, "Now about the treasures. The Coast Guard found an ancient Roman mosaic in one of the containers, and an unusual sword made partly with gold and gemstone in the silt. They're sending both items off to a museum to be studied. They also found hundreds of gold bars in one of the containers, a bunch of geologists and other scientists are examining them to figure out where they came from."

The Chief smiled for the first time continuing. "They aren't the only items that were recovered."

He then opened a desk drawer and pulled out three plastic bags...full of cash, gold coins, jewellery, smartphones and other valuables.

As Megalos looked on in surprise Giorgos continued, "Those treasure hunters really did recover the safe, but they had the contents stolen by Wolfgang afterward. Our divers recovered the items near the broken pieces of Wolfgang's speedboat on the seafloor. The Treasure Rebels told us exactly where to look. Due to water damage the electronic devices are ruined and the physical dollar bills as well, but all the gold and other valuables appear fine. The passengers have been living at the hotel down the street, you can drop by right now with one of my men and have everyone go over the items to ensure the right people get their belongings back."

Megalos lifted the valuables off the desk and thought back on the Treasure Rebels.

"I heard they lost their yacht? Is that true?"

"Wolfgang is responsible for that. We're working to ensure he foots the bill when the Rebels buy a new one."

Megalos nodded his head, "Good. Make him pay."

He then stood and said, "I'd like to thank those three personally for helping me."

"That won't happen."

"Why not?"

"Last I heard they've already left Greece."

==

(One Week Later – Foothills Of Italy – Archaeology Site)
An old grey black Hummer slowly rolled to a stop before a large white tent bordering an archaeology dig. Maddox,

Amber, and Gunnar jumped out while a middle aged woman walked out of the tent.

Dr. Everly Markos was a happy yet tired looking archaeologist in her late forties. She was one of Europe's most well-known scientists...and a descendant of the mysterious Dr. Markos from ancient times.

She and Maddox's father had led an archaeology team throughout Europe and Africa for many years. But tragedy had struck over two and a half years ago when the team accidentally discovered an underground cavern filled with ancient artefacts in northern Africa.

Upon entering the cavern a large nest full of strange insects broke loose from a nearby tree and dropped inside the ancient site. Almost everyone was viciously stung and in the ensuing panic to escape the cavern roof collapsed, crushing or trapping Maddox's father and four members of the team inside. The sixteen who did escape soon dropped to the ground in agony from the bizarre stings.

Every attempt at rescuing the trapped archaeologists proved futile, and with the nest still trapped inside the cavern the doctors could not identify what type of insect was responsible for the bites.

One of the team members, a twenty-something archaeology student named Judy Jagson, discovered one of the odd looking insects had died after stinging her, still stuck to her arm moments before she collapsed. Briefly awakening in the hospital she showed the dead insect to Dr. Everly who instantly recognized the weird looking bug from a written description she had read from a Roman General around 201 A.D. In that same report the General claimed an explorer and doctor named Darius Markos was travelling with his army and had cured his soldiers who had been bitten by the same type of pest.

Studying further, Everly realized Darius Markos was carrying the medicine with him when he had died in Greece. From there the trail went cold.

When two more members of the archaeology team died from the insect stings, she desperately turned to the only person she knew who might be able to track done and locate Dr. Markos' medicine.

She called Maddox Tarver.

Filled with grief about his father's death and knowing many of the people who were struggling to survive from the effects of the insect poison, he decided to help.

His first move was to ask Travis and Amber to join him. They agreed and the Treasure Rebels were born.

Everly hugged Gunnar as she laughed almost in a state of unbelief, "You finally found it!"

Maddox and Amber lifted a black ribbed container the size of a water cooler out of the SUV and set it down. With a flourish they unlocked the latches and opened the lid.

Dozens of bottles containing the same medicine as the vial found in Dr. Markos' wooden box were visible along with the five papyrus pages and ancient instruments.

She stared down at the papyrus papers in disbelief, "Are these really his handwritten notes?"

Maddox grinned, "They're his."

She looked back up saying, "Darius Markos was a soldier turned explorer turned doctor. He was a bit of a philanderer as well, having twin sons from an affair while he stayed in Africa. When he passed away in Greece no-one knew about the two boys or their mother, so his possessions were scattered throughout the Empire."

She then lifted the pages up in awe and continued, "I'm the first descendant to hold something he wrote or owned!"

Gunnar asked directly, "What is the current health status of everyone?"

"Two more went into a coma last week. As it stands eight are in a coma, three are critical, and the rest are still struggling to live normal lives. They're scattered throughout Europe in different hospitals with different treatments but as you know Gunnar none of it has worked."

She then lifted two of the bottles out triumphantly and continued, "But now we have the cure! I'll deliver the medicine personally and immediately to all thirteen here in Europe."

She then looked at them quizzically.

"But what about Judy Jagson in the States?"

===

(Hawaii – Honolulu Hospital)

The weather was perfect. And the only sounds to be heard were the palm tree branches swaying in slow perfect unison and the rolling waters of the beautiful Pacific Ocean.

But the peacefulness was suddenly broken as a black and dark purple Bugatti Chiron hypercar appeared out of the distance. The multimillion vehicle skidded to a stop directly below a flight of steps leading to the hospital's revolving front door, the man at the wheel uncaring if the spot would get him a ticket. He leaped out and ran up the stone steps.

The person at the help desk was a hospital volunteer in his twenties, busily typing a lengthy report into a computer spreadsheet program. He was also a huge boxing fan. Looking up from the screen for just a second, the young man spotted one of the most famous boxers in the world looking down at him. Startled he spit his pumpkin spiced latte all over the keyboard. The young man didn't waste a second cleaning the keys. Instead he jumped up and shook Travis' hand.

"An honour Mr. Jagson! An honour! Welcome back to your home state! How can I help?"

Travis placed a vial of the newly made medicine atop the counter. "I'm here to see my sister."

Five minutes later Travis stepped into a third floor patient's room while the volunteer walked away promising to call in the doctor.

Lying in a bed in a coma was twenty-six year old Judy Jagson, Travis' sister and only family member. She was the reason Travis had given up boxing to join Maddox and Amber in searching the world for Dr. Markos' medicine. Now here he stood holding the cure for Judy's sickness.

He sat down beside her and waited, jumping up when Dr. Williams entered. Shaking the Doctor's hand he explained, "Remember I told you I could bring her out of the coma, get her healed?" He then handed the vial over.

Dr. Williams looked at the vial suspiciously. "What is this? Some New Age alternative treatment?"

"No. It's an old natural medicine."

Williams sighed. He had a long day ahead and as much as he admired Travis' care for his sister, he had gotten tired of hearing from the treasure hunter.

"I appreciate your never ending enthusiasm Mr. Jagson but-"

Travis stopped him by handing over a white envelope containing Gunnar's notes.

Opening the envelope Dr. Williams' eyes widened in surprise as he read the scientific pages. Hands trembling he looked at the vial with new respect.

"I have to verify this."

"Of course. Do it."

The doctor turned back to the pages and kept reading, completely absorbed. He finally looked back at the famous treasure hunter who was now sitting by the bed, holding Judy's hand and studying the digital readings in the medical equipment.

"If this works, she'll be awake later today."

Travis glanced up at Dr. Williams with the biggest smile of his life.

"I know."

PART IX: SPEECHLESS

(One Week Later – Gunnar Monette's Apartment – Miami)

Dr. Monette and the Treasure Rebels were celebrating their victories in Gunnar's sparsely furnished yet warm apartment.

"How is the archaeology team doing?"

"Some are recovering faster than others, but everyone is going to fully recover!"

"Wonderful!"

Gunnar then looked away from Amber and spoke to Travis. "What about Judy?"

"She's going to need four months of physiotherapy to build her strength up, but she's happy."

Travis then pointed back at him, "Chest all good?"

Gunnar smiled, "My lungs have fully recovered from Greece!"

Suddenly he remembered something important and sat down at his computer saying, "I have excellent news! After many hours of extensive searching I've come up with the coordinates for the location of the castle in the drawing you found in the sunken ruins!" He excitedly opened a file and clicked PRINT. The old printer began humming as it warmed up and Gunnar shook his head disgustedly at the delay. "Give it a minute to work properly."

Just then his phone chimed and after reading the incoming text he exclaimed, "I'm so sorry, I must leave." He then stood and shook Travis and Maddox's hands before giving his daughter a hug saying to her, "The meeting time has been pushed forward and I must head downtown. Some of my best friends from my school days are interested in studying Markos' ancient notes. You all enjoy the food without me, and I'll be back in a couple hours."

He then grabbed his coat but paused at the door looking at Travis and Maddox.

"What will you two do now? Look for new treasures? Or try something completely different?"

"I'm flying back to Hawaii tomorrow. Judy and I are going to spend the next few months making up for all the lost time."

"No boxing?"

"Not for now...but I'll maybe enter a few weightlifting competitions I've had my eye on. Be fun for Judy to see me compete."

"You both must come back for Amber's wedding!"

"You bet!"

"What about you?"

Maddox turned away from the printer which had just finished spitting out the page of coordinates and looked up.

"Back racing motorcycles."

Gunnar then opened the door and waved to them all, "Save a little glass of the champagne for me!" With that he was gone and walking to the car garage below.

A moment of quiet passed.

Maddox took off the sunglasses and suddenly getting a little emotional said, 'He's right in a way. Thank you both for agreeing to become Treasure Rebels. You made the last couple years gnarly."

Amber shook her head, "Don't talk like that! You make it sound like a sort of goodbye."

Just then her phone began buzzing loudly. She scooped it off the glass table and noticed the name blinking across the screen. Her fiancé.

She disappeared around the corner into the kitchen chatting happily. Travis lifted his own smartphone up in the air for Maddox to see. "Good time to tell you now. Victoria just missed us at the hospital. On the beach she wanted me to tell you she still cares about you." He then placed the phone on the table and slid it across to Maddox.

"Call her. Just do it." Travis then walked away towards the kitchen. "I'll get some pizza."

Maddox apprehensively examined the phone's screen. A dozen texts were visible, each one clearly from Victoria. He began reading each message, and everything in him wanted to grab the phone and call.

But he hesitated.

In the kitchen Travis spent a half minute opening the pizza box and cutting up a half dozen slices. He then looked at Amber who was still laughing and chatting on the phone.

"You want one?"

She shook her head. No.

"More for me!"

She made a face but that only made him laugh more. He then called out to Maddox in the living room, "Need a drink before you call her?"

But Maddox didn't reply.

Travis closed the pizza box and called out again, "C'mon. You gotta call her!"

Still no response.

A look of slight unease crossed Travis' face. Something felt wrong.

He apprehensively walked back out, "Maddox..."

Maddox was gone.

The printout in the paper tray was missing, and the smartphone was right where Travis had left it, untouched on the centre of the table. One of the balcony sliding glass doors was slightly open.

Amber paused at the sudden silence. The guys were *never* that quiet. She put the phone down for a second and joined Travis who was now standing out on the second floor balcony looking furiously down the street.

"Travis what's wrong! Where's Maddox?"

He shook his head in utter confusion.

"I don't know. He just..." He glanced back at the street and the lit boardwalk by the beach.

She glanced at the printer then noticed the blank computer screen in alarm. Rushing to the keyboard she quickly typed a couple commands. "He took the printout of the castle coordinates and deleted all the computer data!"

Travis looked back down at the busy traffic, his eyes a burning mixture of anger and bewilderment. He hoped to catch a glimpse of his friend or hear the roar of the Triumph motorcycle.

Nothing. Maddox had vanished.

Feeling a sense of loss and dread at the same time he looked back at Amber, "I think Maddox really was tryin' to say goodbye."

===

(Three Days Later – Coast Guard Cutter – Aegean Sea)

The yellow helicopter circled the vessel until finally coming to a rest atop the helo pad. Three crewmen rushed out and secured the wheels with chocks while the pilot cut the engines. The passenger door slid open with a loud crack and Travis and Amber stepped onto the grey deck.

One of the crewmen signalled them to follow him, yelling over the roar of the slowing helo blades, "He's secured at the other end of the ship. He's scheduled to be sent to a European jail later today."

The two treasure hunters followed the crewman to the far end of the ship until they stopped a dozen feet from their greatest enemy.

Wolfgang was sitting on a small metal bench, each of his hands separately handcuffed to the immovable steel. He looked at the two Rebels with bitter resentment as they stood opposite him. The crewman shook their hands and pointed to three officers fully armed standing a hundred yards away. "He can't go anywhere, but just in case we have armed officers ready to neutralize him if he tries to hurt you or escape."

The crewman left and after an awkward quiet Amber began, "We've come to ask a simple question. Who are Tyson and Creggs? You mentioned them on the boat to Maddox."

Wolfgang stared back, his emotionless eyes matching his emotionless face. Finally the anger showed and he snarled, "Ask Maddox."

She hesitated before replying, "We can't. He's disappeared."

Wolfgang's expression of unnerving anger changed to one of unnerving curiosity.

Travis pulled out a photocopy of the jungle castle sketch and explained bluntly, "We found this in the gladiator ruins.

We blew the image up and found the name Creggs handwritten on the bottom corner. Where's the castle?"

Wolfgang just smirked and lowering his head he began examining the handcuffs. He wasn't going to say anything.

Amber and Travis looked at each other. They weren't surprised.

Travis pulled a small envelope out of his back pocket and handed it to Wolfgang as Amber explained, "You are legally obligated to pay us millions of dollars for a new yacht. We'll waive that requirement if you tell us where Maddox is."

Wolfgang looked up and took the envelope, reading the note inside slowly and carefully while they waited for an answer.

After ten seconds passed with no response, she finally lost her patience and asked him directly, "Where is this castle and why is Maddox interested in it?"

Wolfgang's head shot up in surprise, his temper getting the best of him.

"Don't play stupid! You both know Maddox is out to stop Vontaze."

Amber and Travis looked at each other completely baffled. "Who's Vontaze?"

Wolfgang simply stared back at them with chilled annoyance and replied sarcastically.

"You don't know Vontaze? The biggest criminal in Eastern Europe? Of course you both know."

He then stretched his arms in the air as far as the chains would allow then after they dropped back to his sides he irritably continued, "We all know Vontaze can't be beaten. I've never set foot in his castle, and the moment you three do he'll make you disappear like everyone else who tried to steal from him."

Amber stepped closer and declared, "We don't care who Vontaze is! What is it Maddox is trying to steal from him?"

Wolfgang looked back at her shocked at what she had said. He waited a couple seconds, but when he didn't get another response he began to laugh louder and louder as he realized the truth.

With glee he tilted his head back and laughed almost uncontrollably, tears spilling down his grotesque face. He finally turned back at them and mockingly spat between laughs, "You mean...you mean...you both don't know...who Maddox really is?"

They just looked at Wolfgang, bewildered and speechless.

EPILOGUE: THE CASTLE

(Somewhere Along The Mediterranean Coast)

A young nurse climbed the steps towards the top of the castle rampart, where an elderly man sitting in a wheelchair looked over the stone wall at the Mediterranean Sea in the distance. A couple hundred yards away two guards wearing suits leisurely walked along the stone rampart, keeping an eye on the forest of trees below the ancient wall.

She set the tray she was carrying down beside the elderly prisoner.

The old man smiled and nodded to her. On the tray was his breakfast, medicine, medical file and some reading material.

She opened his file and scanned the pages. Most of the medical notes were from long ago but made for incredible reading. It was full of x-rays of broken bones, a report on an eel bite to his left foot, and dozens of other injuries.

She then read the latest report: no significant cognitive decline. She wasn't surprised. The nurse she was replacing had told her the old man, "...must have had every bone and organ in his body injured, except his brain."

Despite his extensive injuries he only needed a couple vitamin pills and a few basic medications. Not bad for someone living as a prisoner for decades.

She looked down at the man. Despite his age his frail shoulders and back were still larger than most men in their prime.

She then looked again at the name. "How are we this morning...*Jacob*?"

"Excellent."

"Jacob" was not his name. But it was the name she had been instructed to call him, not the strange name in his file.

"I'm happy to report your..." He noticed her hesitate. The medical staff weren't supposed to be too nice with the prisoners. That must mean someone unpleasant had stepped onto the rampart.

Sitting more upright "Jacob" slightly turned his aching neck and spotted him. The man in the silver suit. The man who owned the castle. The man no police force could ever catch.

Vontaze.

"Enjoy your breakfast, Jacob. Same as every morning."

"Jacob" didn't reply. He never talked to Vontaze. Not for the last ten years.

Vontaze waited for a reply from his prisoner, but when it didn't come he looked down at his ten thousand dollar watch and strolled back into the dark interior of the castle, his steps to the floor below echoing off the medieval walls. Another moment passed and the nurse relaxed and went back to work preparing the elderly man's breakfast.

"Thank you. I hope Mr. Vontaze treats you and all the staff here well."

She simply nodded her head and replied, "Very well."

As long as we don't try to contact the police on Mr. Vontaze, she thought to herself.

She then grasped the magazines and closed the medical file. She paused as she held onto the old file, her curiosity getting the best of her as she reflected on the name inside.

"I know Jacob isn't your real name...or is it?"

He began chewing some olive bread and replied without looking up, "No! What name have they got written in my file?"

"Just a nickname...Rainforest Rogue."

He smiled, not having heard the name spoken in years.

She continued, "If I may ask, what's your real name then?"

"The file is correct. That is my name."

Completely baffled what to say next, she placed the magazines on the table and said simply, "Here's the reading material you requested for the week."

It was a collection of newspapers, magazines, and archaeology research papers. But she quickly noticed a trend when she scanned the headlines.

"You're a fan of the Treasure Rebels?"

The Rogue smiled and motioned towards the open Mediterranean Sea in the distance, "I love reading about their hunts for treasure!"

She smiled politely and turned to leave but stopped as she noticed something surprising about the front page picture on the top magazine. She pointed at the photo and explained, "You know, "Mr. Rogue," as I look at the picture, if you were quite a bit younger...you would look a lot like him...the one in the sunglasses."

She then continued and pointed towards the sea, "Maybe in the future you will get to spot him and the rest of the Treasure Rebels out there looking for shipwrecks full of gold!"

He grasped the magazine and lifted it up to his old eyes, "Thank you young lady, what a very happy thought!"

She left and headed for the stairs, pleased to have cheered him up. As she disappeared down the winding stairway he continued to stare out at the Mediterranean Sea, still holding the magazine in his shaking hands. His eyes welling up with emotion he looked back down at the photo of Maddox and laughed to himself, "Of course I would look like my grandson!"

Don't miss out!

Visit the website below and you can sign up to receive emails whenever Gerard Doris publishes a new book. There's no charge and no obligation.

https://books2read.com/r/B-A-WRCD-YPDZB

BOOKS 2 READ

Connecting independent readers to independent writers.

Did you love *Greek Gladiator Sharks*? Then you should read *Wrath of the Renegades*[1] by Gerard Doris!

[2]

When the King's royal vessel is savagely attacked in the dead of night by a pirate warship called the "Tombstone Maker," the only survivors must join forces to track the pirates down and rescue their loved ones.

Calling themselves "Honourable Renegades" the four heroes must overcome a horde of enemies, betrayal, and a monstrous creature deep within the Amazon.

---

1. https://books2read.com/u/47kRdN

2. https://books2read.com/u/47kRdN

Loaded with suspenseful action, memorable characters, and exotic jungle locations, *Wrath of the Renegades* is a fast paced and fresh take on the classic pirate genre.

Read more at https://gerarddoristhrillers.com.

Also by Gerard Doris

Treasure Rebels Adventure Novella
Nile River Scorpion
Congo Spider Fangs
Amazon Swamp Victory
India Yeti Pirates
Greek Gladiator Sharks

Standalone
Wrath of the Renegades

Watch for more at https://gerarddoristhrillers.com.

About the Author

Thanks for reading! I write adventure fiction that features treasure hunters, pirates, and renegades. I'm also a fan of NFL football, westerns, classic action movies, and anything that promotes genuine adventure. For some fun updates on my writing projects, you can follow me on X (formerly Twitter) at: @gerard_advfict

Read more at https://gerarddoristhrillers.com.